Stephen replaced the receiver and shuddered.

The feeling Genny needed someone strengthened tenfold. He didn't want to tell her what her sister said.

"She's not coming, is she?"

The tremble in her voice made him ache to gather Genny up in his arms and protect her from further hurt. "Not until tomorrow, but I'm here, and I'm not going anywhere."

Genny's hand found his jaw, her fingers stroking ever so softly over his face. "Thank you."

Stephen placed a gentle kiss in her palm. Something felt so right about being here with her. With that thought, he pulled back. "You need to rest."

She smiled. "I'm too excited. When are they going to bring Jonathan to me?"

Stephen found himself thankful for the low light in the room. "They'll probably let you know before too much longer." He changed the subject quickly. "Genny, I'll have to leave soon. We're performing in Atlanta tonight."

"Oh, Stephen, you'll be exhausted."

"I wouldn't have missed this for a million dollars."

"I love to hear you perform. Jonathan and I will always be your number one fans. We'll scream for your autograph."

Stephen grimaced. "Please don't. It's refreshing to be treated like a regular person."

"But you're not regular," Genny insisted. "You're a gifted man. I have all your CDs."

A smile lifted the corner of his mouth. Fans came in all shapes and sizes. "Thanks for ⬚⬚⬚⬚⬚

"Really, I love your music,⬚⬚⬚⬚⬚ I'm no good with words."

Stephen thought she was⬚⬚⬚⬚⬚ more than any he'd received⬚⬚⬚⬚⬚ You have to rest," he ordered,⬚⬚⬚ kissing her lightly on the forehead. "Good night," he whispered, pleased by the steady breathing that indicated she slept.

TERRY FOWLER makes her home in North Carolina where she works for the city of Wilmington. The second oldest of five children, she shares a home with her best friend who is also her sister. Besides writing, her interests include genealogical research through the Internet and serving her small church in various activities.

Books by Terry Fowler

HEARTSONG PRESENTS
HP298—A Sense of Belonging
HP346—Double Take
HP470—Carolina Pride

Close Enough to Perfect

Terry Fowler

Heartsong Presents

A note from the author:
I love to hear from my readers! You may correspond
with me by writing:

Terry Fowler
Author Relations
PO Box 719
Uhrichsville, OH 44683

ISBN 1-58660-667-0

CLOSE ENOUGH TO PERFECT

All Scripture quotations, unless otherwise indicated, are taken from
the HOLY BIBLE, NEW INTERNATIONAL VERSION®. NIV®. Copyright © 1973,
1978, 1984 by International Bible Society. Used by permission of
Zondervan Publishing House. All rights reserved.

All of the characters and events in this book are fictitious. Any
resemblance to actual persons, living or dead, or to actual events is
purely coincidental.

PRINTED IN THE U.S.A.

one

She stood in semidarkness, engulfed by the deafening roar of fans calling for an encore. Tiny pinpoint flashes of light dotted the arena. These fans were not ready for their evening to end. Cowboy Jamboree didn't let them down.

When the band waved their way offstage for the last time, Genny Smith sighed with relief. She'd enjoyed the concert, but the late hour was catching up with her. Maybe she'd be able to nap on the trip home. Genny doubted that. After meeting the band, the busload of fans would be more exuberant than ever.

"Everyone move this way," the deejay instructed.

Genny could hardly believe she was going backstage. On a whim, she'd dialed the radio station's contest line, never expecting to win gold circle seats and a bus trip to see the CMA group of the year.

Stepping forward, she forced back a gasp at the discomfort that moved through her abdomen. Just as she suspected— eating a carton of Chinese take-out alone had been a mistake. She groaned when another twinge coursed through her.

"You're holding up the line," the guy behind her grumbled.

Doggedly, step by step, Genny forced herself to move. Surely it couldn't be that much farther. Another sharp pain cut through her. As much as she wanted to meet the band, she needed to be home in bed even more.

Each stabbing pain echoed her sister Sonya's sentiments. "Why anyone would subject themselves to a bus ride in the middle of winter to see some country group is beyond me." She'd tacked on "particularly a woman who's six months pregnant" to emphasize her point.

Maybe she should have listened, but Genny really wanted

to see the concert. Her doctor gave her the go-ahead as long as she rested often, didn't take any chances, and wasn't alone. Technically, she wasn't alone. The bus bulged with revelers having the time of their lives.

Soon she would meet Stephen Camden, and then she would find a chair.

❧

People blended together as Stephen listened to yet another fan's praise. Their manager's oft repeated instructions drummed in his head—Show just enough charm to convince them you're sincere. Flirt with the women, slap the men on the back, shake everyone's hand, give them an autograph, say thank you, and move on. The music gives them their money's worth. Anything more is icing on the cake. Ordinarily Stephen hated that philosophy, but tonight he longed for home.

Stephen credited his lingering dissatisfaction to Chuck Harper's visit that afternoon. He'd been less than welcoming when his housekeeper showed the man into his study.

"We've got a once-in-a-lifetime opportunity. I tried to call and kept getting the machine."

Stephen grimaced at Chuck's enthusiasm. "I didn't want to be bothered."

"Steve, Man, this is an honor that can't be refused."

"Some bigger name fall through?" he countered.

Chuck shrugged. "Maybe, but it's a chance to climb another rung on the success ladder. That doesn't hurt Cowboy Jamboree."

"We're tired. We just spent four weeks on the road. We only agreed to tonight's concert because it was close to home."

"That's the biz, Steve."

Stephen glanced at the television, the picture out of focus as he considered how tired he was of his lifestyle. "So you say. We're not programmed for continuous work."

"Steve, Man, what are you griping about? You've got the life men dream about. Nobody telling you what to do."

Other than you, he countered silently.

"No ties."

No one to love. Try another, Stephen thought grimly.

"Different women in every city."

Women who would do anything to be with a celebrity. No thanks. Every time Harper took advantage of another willing victim, Stephen prayed for the man and his family.

"Not to mention tons of money."

What good was money if you didn't have a chance to enjoy the things it bought? I can't hook my home behind the bus.

His lifestyle might be the manager's idea of perfection but it had a long way to go before it matched Stephen's. Right now, all he wanted was to sleep in his own bed and the crucial off time he needed to prepare himself for the next concert tour.

"At least you don't have to listen to a wife and kids nagging on the road."

The man doesn't know how blessed he is. I'd take a lovely, devoted wife and three children any day.

"The way I see it, the only thing a family is good for is a tax deduction," Harper concluded.

That was an idea. If I can't enjoy the lifestyle my money affords me, a wife and family could. "I'd love some of those things you mentioned. Ties, a family to share my life, a reason to come home."

"Don't be so hard on me, Steve. We'll catch a break before the next gig. I promise."

Harper's promises were about as reliable as the man himself. Next time there would be even more reasons why the band couldn't afford to pass up another unplanned opportunity.

"What time do we leave?"

Harper literally beamed his satisfaction. Removing a planner from his expensive suit coat, he ripped out the page and jotted the information. Stephen flinched away from the slap on the back and crammed the paper into the pocket of his well-worn jeans.

In the entry hall, the manager nudged a canvas mailbag with his shoe. "We need to hire someone to take care of these."

No doubt the time had come to talk to the rest of the band. Single and tired, he could only imagine how the others felt.

Forcing himself back to the present, Stephen noted the woman. Her fragile appearance bothered him as did the grimaces that touched her face. What was wrong with these people? She was obviously in trouble.

Of course, he'd long since stopped being surprised by the lack of compassion in others. These fans couldn't care less about one tiny, defenseless woman. He whispered up a quick prayer for her care.

He waved Kyle, the roadie who doubled as a bodyguard, off and stepped forward. "Hello, Beautiful." Stephen glanced at the backstage pass and saw her name was Genny. He had the distinct feeling he'd been punched in the stomach when her lips curved into a smile and her hand rested in his. She groaned, her knees buckling.

Stephen regarded the woman in his arms. He'd never had a fan faint before. This one was limp as an overcooked noodle and about as heavy. He sought her pulse and sighed with relief at the steady, if weak, beat.

"Somebody get a doctor," he called, looking around for a place to lay her down. People crowded the area and short of knocking the refreshments off the table, there didn't appear to be anywhere to put her. He swung her up into his arms.

"Steve, what are you doing?" Harper demanded.

"I'm not putting her on the floor."

"Don't be a fool. Leave her to the people she came with."

"Do you see anyone, Harper? Either help or get out of the way."

"She can sue us, Steve."

Obviously the man had never heard of the Good Samaritan. She needed someone and apparently he was the chosen one. "I accept complete responsibility. Will it jeopardize Kyle if he holds the door?"

The roadie cleared the way. "Where are you taking her?"

Cameras flashed all around them, and Stephen did his best

to shield her. "To the bus."

"It's your skin," Harper called.

"Shout a little louder," Steve muttered. "There's a reporter over in the corner who didn't hear you." He whispered a prayer for forgiveness for his anger.

The long duster coat he wore on stage protected Stephen from the cold January night. The woman wore a dress that couldn't be all that warm and a long sweater. Where was her coat? Protectively, he tucked her closer.

Steve waited for Kyle to unlock the bus and carried her to the bed in the back. He reached for a throw and spread it over Genny. As the folds settled in place, her eyes fluttered open.

"Hello. Are you okay?"

She closed her eyes and opened them again. "I don't know."

He watched her closely. *Okay, God, I could use some help here.*

❧

She watched his thorough assessment and knew what he saw—mousy, shoulder-length brown hair badly in need of a trim, green eyes outlined by dark circles, and the swollen puffiness that distorted her entire body. Her largest dress fit snugly about her stomach and had seen better days. *What a mess he must think me.*

He looked younger than on his album covers, handsomer. His thick brown hair showed a liberal mixture of red highlights and nearly touched his shoulders. His shoulders strained against the long denim coat he wore, and his haunting gaze all but bored into her.

Her fascination lessened when her body reminded Genny of her dilemma. She rolled onto her side and found the position even more uncomfortable. She moved her hands protectively over her stomach.

"What's wrong?"

"I'm having sharp pains."

"A virus? Something you ate?"

Genny considered her gluttony. A number of foods hadn't agreed with her pregnancy.

"I hope it's not food poisoning," he said. "One of our guys said he'd never been so sick in his life."

She knew the feeling. She wanted to curl up and die but even that required too much effort right now.

"Can I get you some medicine? We have stuff in the first aid kit."

"I can't."

He settled on the edge of the bed, holding her hand in his. "Right. When's the baby due?"

Genny told him. "My doctor warned me to take things easy. I'm thirty-six years old." Why had she told him that? He wasn't interested in the facts of her pregnancy, nor the facts of her life for that matter.

❧

Stephen watched the apologetic smile disappear. "Are you here alone?"

Silence filled the room. Her fingers plucked at the throw. *Way to go, Man.* "Don't be afraid," he reassured. "I just thought that in your condition you shouldn't be alone. Where's your husband?" Stephen hesitated. "The baby's father."

She stared at him through uncomprehending eyes. "John?" Her voice sounded disembodied.

"Yes. John," he urged. "Where is he? How can we contact him?"

"He's gone."

The pinched whiteness of her face scared him. "Gone where?"

"I didn't know there would be a fire." Her voice caught suddenly, revealing a deep hurt within her. "If I hadn't told him to finish his work. . ."

The nightmare worsened. "I'm sorry." Stephen grabbed a tissue and wiped away the tears easing along her soft skin.

Despite her pregnancy, she was skin and bones. A strong urge to protect her pulled at Stephen. He continued to whisper words of comfort.

❧

Genny felt strengthened by Stephen's nearness.

The warm cocoon did nothing to block out the damp cold of the winter night or the whine of the gusting wind. The clouds released the rain that had threatened all day. Almost deafening, it pummeled the bus. Genny felt more than a little thankful she wasn't braving the elements. Feeling warm, she pushed the throw to the side.

Stephen pulled it back into place. "It's cold in here."

"Not to me."

"Even more reason. Do you have a fever?" He touched the back of his hand to her forehead.

Genny wiped perspiration from her face. "It's the pain. I splurged on Chinese food this afternoon. Maybe I just ate too much. Do you. . . ? Could we call a doctor?"

He jumped up. "Let me see what I can do. Wait, you have to tell me your last name."

"Genny Smith. Actually it's Genevieve," she admitted with an embarrassed smile.

"I like it."

"I never have."

He disappeared, and Genny tried and discarded every relaxation trick she knew. Not even the usually soporific tendencies of falling rain could induce sleep.

Nothing seemed capable of overpowering the nagging pains that plagued her. Surely they would go away after a good night's rest. Stubbornly, Genny snuggled under the blanket and squeezed her eyes shut.

❧

He beat a hasty retreat up the aisle of the bus and found Kyle in the driver's seat, staring glumly at the rain running in rivulets down the windshield.

The roadie looked almost relieved to see him. "Man, you won't believe the mess out there. Some idiot caused a pileup that's blocked all the outgoing lanes."

"Can we get out?"

"It's not going to happen for awhile. Can't find the group that brought her in either. We think they left her. You should take her back inside, Steve. You don't need the liability."

"She's not facing this alone."

Kyle shrugged, and his words echoed the manager's. "It's your neck."

When she called out to him, Stephen thought something about her voice didn't match the woman. She certainly wasn't beautiful, not like other women he knew. But her voice—now that was a promise of heaven. He could listen to her say his name again and again. And those eyes—huge and as green as a spring forest.

His next thought surprised him. *Oh, come on, Man. It's just wishful thinking on your part.*

Stephen found Genny sobbing softly, her face turned into the pillow. He reached for her hand. "We don't mean to upset you."

"You didn't. Pregnancy has made me more emotional. I cry at the drop of a hat."

Stephen grinned, entranced by the cadence of her voice. As a singer, he knew the voices that made the big bucks. "You have a fabulous voice. Do you sing along with the band when you hear us on the radio?"

Her strangled laughter produced the same lilting quality. "Please, my singing is your worst nightmare."

"You have a beautiful voice."

"They wouldn't even let me into the church choir."

He laughed. "Oh, come on. It can't be that bad. They let everybody sing in church."

"Why don't I regale you with. . . Ow," she grunted. "Noooo!"

"What? What is it?" he demanded anxiously.

"I think my water broke."

Tears flooded her eyes. Stephen whispered comforting remarks as he tucked a lock of her hair behind her ear. "Shush. Don't cry. Who's your doctor?"

"Rainer." She recited the number from memory.

Stephen raced up the aisle.

"What happened? Why is she screaming?"

Stephen forced himself to remain calm. "I think we're about to deliver a baby."

"I'm out of here. Vick just radioed to say the guys are ready to call it a night. I told him there was a traffic jam, but he says they're tired of the crowd and want to come on board."

"Tell them to come on. A couple of the guys have experience in the delivery room. And grab a cell phone."

"Man, are you crazy?"

Doubt filled Stephen. Was he taking unnecessary chances? Maybe. But if he didn't take care of her, who would? "Hang on, Kyle. It's going to be a rough ride."

"Hey, Man, I'm going to see if there are any paramedics in the building. Chances are they're all down at the accident scene."

"Do what you can. I'm going back to her."

❧

Genny bit her lip as the pain tore through her. The doctor had said most first-time mothers were in labor for several hours, but he hadn't prepared her for this. Perhaps she should have read all the literature they gave her. She thought she had time. Some lesson in procrastination.

The silence weighed like a heavy blanket. Genny couldn't hear what they were saying this time. Where was the ambulance? Dr. Rainer had mentioned stopping early labor. Oh, why hadn't she listened? "Stephen?"

❧

Her cry reminded Stephen she had even more reason than he did to be afraid. "I'm here. Just relax, and tell me what you're feeling."

Genny grabbed his hand. "I'm not due for three months. I can't lose him. He's all I have."

He grew still at the whispered pleas. Stephen realized she was praying in earnest and joined in, sending up his own request. Stephen knew they shared the hope God would bring Genny and the baby safely through this frightening experience.

"Okay, now take a deep breath," he instructed.

Her fingers clutched his hand, her thumb rubbing idly against the callus from his guitar playing. "Dr. Rainer warned me. He's been warning me ever since. . ." Her voice cracked and strengthened. "I tried to take care of my baby. Honestly I did."

"I know, Honey. You did everything you could."

"I tried to eat right, and I stayed in bed until he said the crisis was past. My baby is all I have left."

He hugged her, and Genny's arms slipped about his neck, her head resting on his shoulder as her stomach fit itself to his side. The tremble of her pathetically thin shoulders wrenched his heart, and her suffering became his.

After a moment or so, he took Genny's face in his hands and looked deep into her eyes. "Stop now. This isn't helping. The guys will bring a cell phone, and we'll call your doctor. He can talk us through this."

"I've been so afraid," she said simply.

The whispered words grabbed at his heart. "I'm here now. We're not going to let anything happen to you or your baby."

"How are you doing?"

Her inquiry struck him as odd. "What do you mean?"

"Just wondering how you feel about this nightmare you've landed yourself smack in the middle of."

"I'm not thinking about me right now. You don't have any family?"

"A sister, Sonya."

"Why isn't she with you?"

"Her job demands all her time. I couldn't ask her to do more for me."

A distinct fuzziness crept in her voice as exhaustion took its toll. The quiet made Stephen wonder if she slept.

Couldn't ask for more. The words echoed in his head. Why should she have to ask? If she were his sister, he'd be there for her.

What would he do if this baby opted to make an immediate appearance? He glanced toward the door. Where were the guys with that cell phone?

Stephen knew the pain had worsened by her movements and the clutch of her hand. "Tell me what's happening."

"My baby's coming. Stephen," she began, pushing the request out with her next breath, "will you stay with me?"

"Of course I will."

"I mean if we get to the hospital."

"They won't let me."

"They'll think you're my coach."

Did she realize what she asked of him?

"Stephen, I'm scared. It's as though I have no control over my body. Over the pain."

"Yes, you do." Fear, mainly of failure, had been part of his life for years. Like him, Genny needed reassurance, help getting through this situation. And though he was scared of failing her, Stephen knew he had to give her his all.

Exhaustion showed in her voice. "In a minute."

A few minutes of uninterrupted quiet passed, and Stephen reflected on Genny's fear. Her baby was coming early, and she was stranded with strangers. She must be terrified.

"Stephen, I don't want to pressure you," she whispered.

He saw no reason why she should go through this alone—particularly if she needed him. Very few things had ever been asked of him in life, and this was something he could do. "If I can, I'll stay."

two

Stephen paused, his gaze stopping on the isolette labeled Baby Boy Smith. He couldn't quite believe he had witnessed this child's birth. If the tiny baby wasn't proof enough, he had only to look down at the regulation surgical gown the hospital staff insisted he wear when visiting the nursery.

The previous hours were a blur. Once the entire band and crew became involved, Kyle recruited volunteers to find an ambulance and two band members remained, passing on information to Genny's doctor via the cell phone. Things went into fast motion after help arrived.

Stephen assumed Genny would forget about him, but she held on tightly. When the baby made its appearance, the EMT wrapped her son in a towel and placed him in Stephen's arms.

"He's so tiny," Genny whispered, her gaze following the baby's every movement. "And perfect."

Though weak, she enthused over his features, making Stephen count and admire miniature fingers and toes. Well, she hadn't actually forced him. From that shared moment the strangest feeling came over him, almost as if he should be passing cigars around.

That same feeling rushed through him now as the wrinkled scrap of humanity squalled in earnest. This tiny baby boy would provide so much love and joy to someone who needed it desperately. Stephen wiped moisture from his eyes, a sheepish smile touching his lips when the nurse closed one eyelid in a knowing wink.

He whispered a prayer of thanks. Born at least three months premature, with no doctor or hospital equipment to support him—God's hand was all over this miracle. The human side of him rated the baby's odds of survival as low.

16

The believer knew God was in control. The small baby, with skin so thin Stephen could see veins and arteries, made his presence known with a mewl of protest.

Genny amazed him. Despite the problems, she fought to give her child every chance. Stephen considered how she'd held on with all her might—right up to a couple of minutes ago when the doctor asked him to leave the room.

"How is my baby? Is everything all right?" she demanded.

Something in the man's expression warned Stephen the news wasn't good. His respect for the doctor increased measurably as he calmed Genny.

"How is my son? Is he okay?" she repeated.

"He's being taken care of. I'm more concerned with you."

With a nod, the doctor indicated Stephen should leave the room. After a couple of halting steps, he turned and looked at Genny. Her sad expression stopped him in his tracks. Walking back to the bed, Stephen reached for her hand. "I'll be back. I promise."

Stephen left the nursery window and paced the corridor outside the small waiting room, amazed and fascinated by the turn of events that had taken him from greeting a group of fans to witnessing the birth of a baby.

Harper was furious. The manager sent word to the bus driver that he wanted them on the road immediately. Instead, Stephen went to the hospital with a woman who made him feel the strangest things.

He really should leave. She didn't need him now. Stephen swept a hand through his hair and sighed. He couldn't do that to her. Okay, so maybe she was emotional, but he'd made a promise.

Hoping to catch his friend and fellow band member, Stephen found a pay phone and dialed Ray's cell number.

"Steve? Hold on. Hey, quiet down. Where are you?"

"Looks like I'll be tied up here for awhile."

"The guys won't appreciate a wild-goose chase."

Stephen felt torn. He owed the guys a lot more than he

owed Genny Smith. But it went beyond debts. Genny made him feel needed. Something he hadn't felt in a long time.

Not even with the crowds. He gave a good concert in return for the money, but the experience no longer moved him.

"I'll charter a flight. Leave at the last possible moment."

"Why?" Ray asked.

Genny's vision lingered in Stephen's head. She had no one—only a tiny baby in an isolette. He needed to be there for her. *Crazy.* He shook his head to clear the fog. Stephen flexed his hand, felt the lingering soreness from Genny wrenching it with every contraction and said, "Because I'm needed."

"Okay, Buddy. See you when you get here."

"Thanks, Ray." He glanced up and saw the nurse pointing in his direction. "Gotta go."

He hung up and walked to the desk.

Genny's doctor appeared distracted as he fingered his stethoscope.

"How is she?"

"Are you a friend of hers?"

Stephen explained the events that had brought him to the hospital.

"I hoped you were a friend. I talked to her doctor. He said this woman has had too many shocks in the past few months."

"Will she be okay?"

"In time. She's had a high-risk pregnancy, aggravated by her age and the loss of her husband. Her doctor seemed surprised she survived a regular delivery. He planned cesarean."

A disconcerted smile crinkled the corners of Stephen's eyes. "Thanks for not sharing that a couple of hours ago."

"I don't know how, but you worked a miracle. That tiny boy wouldn't have survived if she'd been alone."

"Not me. God."

"Definitely. She's going to need all the support she can get. Her son will be in NICU for awhile."

"He's. . . ?" The words choked in Stephen's throat.

"No. No. He's stable right now, but Mrs. Smith will be

upset, and it's not good for her or the baby. She'll blame herself, and nothing will change her mind until she accepts and deals with what's happened."

"I wondered. . . I sensed that she's. . . Well, how much more can she take?"

"I wish I knew. From what her doctor said, grief has taken its toll on her emotional and physical state."

Stephen knew without a doubt he wouldn't leave Genny without the support she needed. "I'd like to see her again."

"She's waiting for you."

Stephen pushed the door open and focused on the sleeping woman. In the shadowy light, her face rivaled the white of the sheets. She looked so small, defenseless. And yet, appearances could be deceiving. She had been strong and determined to bring her son, a baby barely as large as his hand, into the world.

Stephen prayed the determination would carry Genny through the turmoil ahead. He sat in the chair by the bed and waited.

"John?" Genny moaned as she woke, her eyes searching the room.

Stephen flashed her a reassuring smile. "Hi, Beautiful. How're you feeling?"

"Terrible," she admitted, groaning softly as she moved. The heavy lashes that shadowed her cheeks flew up. "Stephen? You're still here?"

"I promised."

"Do I really have a son?"

A big grin covered his face. "A very tiny baby boy."

"Is he all right?" Anxiety edged her voice.

Careful, Steve, he admonished. "I figure any baby tough enough to be born in an ambulance during a storm will grow to be a bear of a man."

"I couldn't have done it without you," she whispered.

He smoothed Genny's bangs from her forehead and found himself wishing he could drive the sadness from her eyes. "You did great, Genny. You were so brave."

"I was scared," she admitted, tears welling as she spoke the truth.

Brushing the moisture from her cheek, Stephen said, "Me too. What's his name?"

A slow smile crept over her face. "When we discussed names, John said if it was a boy, he wouldn't be a Junior. He hated the disbelieving stares when he told people his name was John Smith. He suggested Jonathan. "

"And a girl?"

"Pocahontas."

Stephen laughed with Genny.

"Stephen?" she called drowsily.

He gave his support in the only way he knew how, wrapping her hand in both of his as his elbows rested on the bed. "Right here."

"Do you have a middle name? I'd like to name my son after you."

"It's Andrew, but don't you think you should name him after his father?"

"I'm going to name him Jonathan Andrew. That is, if you don't mind?" she said, almost anxiously.

"I'd be honored." The warmth of his smile echoed in the sincerity of his voice. He kissed her forehead. "Get some sleep."

"Did you see him again?" she asked, her voice barely audible from exhaustion.

"He's a beautiful boy."

"Does Sonya know?"

Sonya? The sister that couldn't be there, Stephen realized. "How do I contact her?"

Genny gave him the number, and Stephen dialed. "Is this Sonya Kelly? Yeah, I know it's late, but congratulations, Auntie. Mother and son are doing fine." Stephen squeezed Genny's hand and winked. "She's in the hospital here in Memphis."

"How stupid can one woman be?" Sonya demanded angrily. "I told her not to go on that bus tour. Who are you anyway?"

Her response shocked him. "A friend. We met at the con-cert." He shook his head when Genny reached for the phone. "Baby Jonathan was very unexpected."

Another long sigh preceded Sonya's next words. "Tell her I'll bring her things tomorrow."

Stephen replaced the receiver and shuddered. The feeling Genny needed someone strengthened tenfold. He didn't want to tell her what her sister said.

"She's not coming, is she?"

The tremble in her voice made him ache to gather Genny up in his arms and protect her from further hurt. "Not until tomorrow, but I'm here, and I'm not going anywhere."

Genny's hand found his jaw, her fingers stroking ever so softly over his face. "Thank you."

Stephen placed a gentle kiss in her palm. Something felt so right about being here with her. With that thought, he pulled back. "You need to rest."

She smiled. "I'm too excited. When are they going to bring Jonathan to me?"

Stephen found himself thankful for the low light in the room. "They'll probably let you know before too much longer." He changed the subject quickly. "Genny, I'll have to leave soon. We're performing in Atlanta tonight."

"Oh, Stephen, you'll be exhausted."

"I wouldn't have missed this for a million dollars."

"I love to hear you perform. Jonathan and I will always be your number one fans. We'll scream for your autograph."

Stephen grimaced. "Please don't. It's refreshing to be treated like a regular person."

"But you're not regular," Genny insisted. "You're a gifted man. I have all your CDs."

A smile lifted the corner of his mouth. Fans came in all shapes and sizes. "Thanks for buying them."

"Really, I love your music," she protested. "It's so. . . Oh, I'm no good with words."

Stephen thought she was. In fact, he enjoyed her praise

more than any he'd received in a long time. "Enough talking. You have to rest," he ordered, tucking the sheet about her and kissing her lightly on the forehead. "Good night," he whispered, pleased by the steady breathing that indicated she slept.

three

Genny came awake slowly, feeling disoriented as she tried to focus her gaze. A hand flew to her no longer pregnant form. She had a son. A slow smile crept over her face as the door opened to admit the doctor.

"Good morning, Mrs. Smith. How are you feeling?"

"Dr. Garner, where is my baby? Why didn't they bring him to me?"

His pat on the arm served more to irritate than console.

"Where is my baby?" she repeated, more insistently than before.

Sonya burst into the room and snapped, "What are you carrying on about now?"

"I want to see my baby." The words turned into a sob.

Sonya set a small suitcase on the end of the bed. "Oh, Genny, hush."

"They haven't bought him to me at all."

"In good time. First, we examine you, and then another doctor will talk to you about your baby."

Her gaze focused on the doctor. "Can't I feed him this morning?"

"I'm afraid not. He's in the neonatal care unit."

Genny crumpled, tears flooding her eyes as she pleaded with him. "He'll be all right, won't he?"

"Certainly. But we must be certain you're healthy enough to take your son home. You had a very difficult delivery, and if Mr. Camden hadn't been there, there's a good chance neither of you would have survived."

Stephen. She wished he were here now. All man, from the top of his head to the soles of the expensive cowboy boots, he made her feel safe and secure, happy even. She vaguely

23

recalled him saying he had to be in Atlanta. "Did Stephen get off all right?"

"How should I know?" Sonya snapped. "Where did you find him anyway? He actually thought I'd drive up here last night."

Genny closed her eyes. Her only sister couldn't be bothered to drive a couple of hours to see her nephew.

"I've got to get to work. I'll get back when I can."

Sonya's words were cut off as the door closed behind her. Why couldn't Sonya understand? She hadn't even mentioned the baby.

She probably hadn't realized who Stephen was either. No doubt Sonya would have been there in record time if she'd known.

A thank-you note would never be enough for all he'd done. Perhaps she could repay him one day. Of course naming her son after him was high reward.

"Mrs. Smith," the doctor called impatiently.

"Sorry. What did you say?"

He scowled and continued, "I said a nurse will take you to the nursery to see your child. I. . ."

"Jonathan," she interrupted. "His name is Jonathan Andrew."

He nodded. "I want you to talk with Dr. Lee. Here he is now."

A stranger introduced himself and launched into a summary of Jonathan's case. "Your son is approximately twelve weeks premature, weighing in at 1563 grams." Noting her confusion, he gave the weight in pounds. "He's in what we classify the low birth weight group. Less than 2500 grams but more than 1500 grams, which is good since around 95 percent of those babies survive their newborn period with no future problems."

He droned on, his diagnosis almost too much to absorb. Certain words jumped out at Genny—Isolette. Sepsis workup. Infection. Antibiotics.

Dr. Garner stepped forward, his hand covering hers. "I know it's a lot to take in, but we have very high expectations

or Jonathan. I'm sure Dr. Lee is more than happy to answer
any questions you might have."

The other doctor nodded as Genny's eyes drifted from one
to the other. "What will I do?"

"Just love him."

"You can't imagine how much," she responded softly.

In the nursery, Genny half listened as the nurse outlined the
procedures for scrubbing and provided her with a gown to wear.

The nurse led her over to the isolette. "I'm Cindy. I take
care of Jonathan during first shift."

Awestruck, Genny gazed at her son. "Isn't he beautiful?
What do I do?"

"Put your hands through the portholes and touch him gently. Don't worry so much about the IV," Cindy instructed.

"I'll hurt him."

"It's okay. Really. He needs your touch, and you'll be surprised by how quickly he learns to recognize his mommy's
voice."

Genny's hand trembled as she traced one finger along the
diminutive arm.

"That's good. Relax," Cindy said.

"Why is he wearing the hat?"

"To retain body heat."

"What about the wires?"

"Monitor leads. See that machine? It shows his breathing
and heartbeat. If it gets too high or low, an alarm goes off."

Genny smiled when Jonathan grasped her finger in his tiny
hand. She glanced at the next incubator. "Where's her mother?"

"That little lady isn't as lucky as your Jonathan. Her mom's
in a coma. Her father's military, and we're waiting for the Red
Cross to get him here."

An alarm went off, and horror filled Genny. "What is that?"
she demanded, her heart racing.

"The other baby's monitor. Spend a few minutes with
Jonathan while I take care of her."

The thump of her heart barely slowed as Genny stared at

the monitors attached to Jonathan's frail body. She had done this to him. She'd forced Jonathan to suffer for her weaknesses. A trail of tears chased each other down her cheeks.

"It's okay," Cindy whispered, rubbing Genny's back. "Let's get you back to your room. You can come anytime you want."

Once settled in bed, Genny gave vent to the overwhelming fear. Trembling encompassed her, and the tears flowed steadily. The telephone rang, and she groped for the receiver, brushing at her cheeks before she called hello.

"How are you feeling today?"

The undeniably male voice was unfamiliar at first. "Stephen? Oh, it's so good to hear your voice."

"Hold on a sec."

She could hear him speaking, almost angrily, to someone in the background. "I said I'll be there when I finish my call. Okay, I'm back. What were you saying?"

"Sounds like you're busy."

"Genny, don't hang up."

The urgency in his voice kept her on the line. "But you're busy."

He overrode her protests. "Tell me about Jonathan. How is he?"

"I don't know," she admitted. "He's so tiny. I can't hold him. There are all these wires. His doctor said something about an infection and antibiotics." Her guilt increased with each bit of information. "It's my fault, Stephen. I'm his mother, and he's suffering because of me."

"It's not. Genny, Honey, listen to me. Who's there with you?"

"No one. I'm okay."

A heavy sigh filled the receiver. "You're not. They expect you to grasp the significance of what's going on with your son after you've gone through a horrible ordeal."

"I have to. I'm all he has." Genny sniffed. "I painted this rosy picture of myself leaving the hospital with a healthy child. Now I'm going home alone. I don't even know how long he'll have to stay." She trailed off as the new worry occurred to her. "How will I get to the hospital?"

"Jonathan needs you more than that rosy-cheeked image ever did."

"What if I lose him?"

"We are not going to think that way."

We. With one word, Stephen made her feel protected. "You'll never know how frightened I was when I realized I was in labor."

"Not half as much as me. It certainly isn't an experience I'd care to try again anytime soon."

"I hope I didn't put you off becoming a father."

"Aren't I going to be an honorary uncle?" he asked. "Unofficially of course."

"Officially," Genny said. "If you give me an address, I'll send pictures."

"I'd take you up on a visit," he suggested.

"We'd love to see you."

"Soon then. Take care. And my best to Jonathan."

Genny turned off the phone. He'd soothed so many of her fears. Stephen was a special man. Not many people would put themselves out for a stranger.

And she was going to get a second chance to tell him so. Genny smiled as she drifted off to sleep.

❧

Stephen dug his wallet from his pocket. "Go on without me. I have another call to make."

"Just wrap it up quick and get downstairs," Harper ordered.

Stephen's frustration only made him angrier. How could her sister not be there to help? Such selfishness was mind-boggling.

Stephen had missed a friend's cry for help once, and it resulted in a senseless loss. He vowed it wouldn't happen again. One tiny baby boy wouldn't be all Genevieve Smith had.

Making the decision to help brought him great satisfaction. Maybe part of it was the need to reassure himself, but he suspected there was more to it than that.

Stephen thumbed through the papers in his wallet until

he found his pastor's business card. Glancing at his watch, he dialed the home number. Hopefully Pastor Carl hadn't gone out.

"Hello, Carl. How are you?" he said when the preacher answered on the second ring.

"I'm fine, Stephen. And you? Are you in town?"

"Doing great. We're in Atlanta. I need to ask a favor. There's a young woman by the name of Genevieve Smith at the hospital. Her son was born prematurely, and she's really struggling. I wondered if you could go by and offer comfort? She and her son need our prayers."

"Genevieve Smith," the pastor repeated. "I'll visit her tomorrow."

"Thanks. It's a strange case. From what I know, her husband died recently. She has a sister, but the woman obviously isn't interested in helping out. Do you think some of our churchwomen might visit? I'd like to be there for her, but we're out of town for the next couple of days."

"I'll contact Mrs. Bellamy. She'll set the prayer chain into motion and round up volunteers. We'll take care of Mrs. Smith for you."

Stephen felt thankful that the minister didn't ask further questions. "I really appreciate this. I can't believe her sister could be so selfish."

"Let's not judge, Stephen. Perhaps circumstances make it unavoidable. Either way, we should pray for the sister as well."

"You'd think family would be more important."

"Most people take family for granted," Pastor Carl pointed out. "Have you thought about the matter we discussed?"

Stephen fiddled with the pens on the desktop. "All the time. I can't help but feel I'd be letting everyone down. Some of the guys have families. What would they do until they found a replacement?"

"You could continue until they find someone."

"I considered that. Perhaps I'm a coward."

"As always, pray for God's guidance, Stephen. He will light

your path. Is Mrs. Smith a Christian?"

Stephen didn't know. They had spent hours together, and he honestly had no idea. "I hope so. She's going to need God's strength to get her past this hurdle. I'll see you in church the first Sunday I'm home."

"I'll look forward to seeing you. Meanwhile, we'll take care of Mrs. Smith for you."

Stephen thanked the pastor again and hung up. He was thankful, but something niggled at him. Some reason why he wasn't totally contented with the action he'd taken.

Stephen headed downstairs, stopping by the entrance as the truth hit him. He didn't want other people seeing to Genny's care. He wanted to take care of her.

four

At times, the experience of motherhood overwhelmed Genny, but she coped, forming an undeniable bond with her son. She examined him every visit, in awe of each perfect feature. At first, his tiny size worried her, but she soon learned to convert grams to ounces and began to ask questions. She stored away tidbits of information to share with Stephen.

Genny didn't find it strange that she would think of him. Every time someone from his church stopped by to check on her and Jonathan, to see if she needed anything, or to pray with her, she thanked God. Stephen called every day to offer support and reassurance. Mostly, he made her feel special, Genny admitted, glancing at the yellow roses he'd sent—her favorites.

She battled the strong temptation to share her burdens and found herself placing them in God's hands. Stephen's care and that of his congregation confirmed her faith that God would provide.

"Hello, Mrs. Smith. How are you feeling today?"

Genny missed the familiarity of her regular doctor but found Dr. Garner to be a pleasant substitute. "Fine."

The man flipped pages on her chart, pausing now and then to scribble on them. "You're doing remarkably well. I'm going to release you in the morning, but you have to promise to take things easy."

A knot formed in her stomach. "But what about Jonathan? Will Dr. Lee allow me to move him to Nashville?"

"He feels it's best that Jonathan stays here. I was able to extend your stay a few days, but we've run out of time. Have you checked into family quarters?"

Something else demanding money she didn't have. "I can

stay in the waiting area."

"No," he said sharply. "You have to rest, Mrs. Smith."

"But my son needs me."

The doctor jammed his hand deep into the pocket of his white coat. "He needs you well and able to take care of him. Talk to your family. I'm sure you'll find a way."

Resigned, Genny called and left a message on Sonya's machine before making her way to the nursery. It was bedtime by the time Sonya got around to returning her call.

"I suppose you're wondering why I haven't been to see you?" Sonya went on about work and how there hadn't been a moment to spare.

"I'm being released in the morning," Genny said when Sonya paused for breath.

"You couldn't have picked a more inconvenient time to have a baby. What's the latest I can pick you up?"

"But I need to be here for Jonathan. Is there any way for me to stay?" Genny expected the sarcastic laughter.

"Just come home, Genny. The nursing staff can take care of the baby."

The baby. Why did Sonya never call Jonathan by name? "I'll be ready," Genny said, pushing the words past her tears. Life was so unfair. If only John were alive.

Early the next morning, Genny made a trip to the nursery before going back to her room to sign the discharge papers. When the volunteer wheeled her downstairs, Sonya loaded Genny and her things into the car and drove away without a backward glance.

As usual, the conversation quickly dwindled to silence. Genny wished Sonya would say something to take her mind off the separation. How would she survive without seeing Jonathan daily?

At the condo, Sonya parked and left the engine running. "Come on, Genny," she snapped, holding the door open. "I've got to go to work."

Genny fought back a wave of dizziness when Sonya rushed

her up the walkway to the door.

Inside, Sonya swung the suitcase onto the armchair and sorted out a gown and robe. "Put these on while I get what you need." She disappeared up the stairs and returned with an armload of linens and a pillow. "Hopefully, I'll be home no later than six." Sonya checked the tiny diamond-crusted watch face. "Of course, I'm so far behind now I'll probably never catch up."

Disheartened, Genny sank down on the sofa. She supposed Sonya loved her, but there was a lot of their parents in her sister. Always on the go, much too busy for anyone but herself. Her sibling was the beautiful, self-sufficient one who never lacked for companionship.

They were complete opposites. Shy, skinny, almost mouse-like, Genny preferred to stay inside and read when Sonya was with her friends. They had been cruel to the little girl, telling her to get lost, to find her own friends. With no one to help build her self-esteem, keeping to herself became the solution. Some of the shyness disappeared with maturity, but for the most part she was still a loner who hated being alone.

Genny touched her cheek and realized she was indulging in yet another bout of depression. *Silly,* she berated, *drying her face. I will do better,* Genny vowed, going into the kitchen to prepare lunch.

Not that Sonya left much to prepare. Genny's search yielded half a glass of milk that surprisingly enough hadn't soured since the date was past that stamped on the carton. Scrambling the one egg and toasting the end slice of the bread loaf, she wondered if Sonya would make it home for dinner. Even then she'd probably be tired and want to order in.

Genny cleared the kitchen and went back into the living room to make her bed on the sofa. Tired, she dozed in a restless sleep, coming awake slowly upon realizing there was someone at the door.

Stephen flashed her a smile that set her heart to racing. "I woke you."

She became instantly alert, too surprised to do more than nod. The old, familiar warmth of security surrounded her as she recognized someone who cared. Genny took his arm. "Come in. When did you get back?"

She glanced at the sofa. The armchair held her suitcase and articles Sonya had thrown from her case. "Sorry," Genny exclaimed and started to move the linen.

Stephen looked pointedly toward the makeshift bed. "You were asleep? I should have phoned."

"You're always welcome," Genny emphasized. "How did you know where to find me?"

"Let's just say it doesn't hurt to be well-known."

Why was she so happy to see him? They were friends. At least she hoped so. "I'm surprised. I know you said soon but. . ."

"I got back earlier than expected. How are you feeling?"

"Fine." At his doubtful look, she laughed. "Well, as good as any woman who has just given birth is allowed to feel."

Stephen nodded. "Have you eaten?"

"Yes. I'd offer you something but I just bared the cupboards. Sonya's going to have to grocery shop. She'll hate that. She hasn't been since I came here to live."

"Did you have enough?"

"It'll hold me."

He frowned when her traitorous stomach rumbled in denial. "I bought you something." Stephen passed her a gift-wrapped package she hadn't seen earlier.

"You shouldn't have." Genny tore into the present. A sigh of pleasure slipped from her as she drew out a silky, crush-proof dress in a gorgeous shade of green.

"I hope it fits. I told the saleswoman you barely weighed a hundred pounds, were about so high, and had just had a baby. She showed me this dress. Picking the color was easy. It's the same as your eyes."

"It's beautiful. But you shouldn't have."

Their gazes locked, tenderness growing in his eyes with his smile. "There's more. Under the dress."

The second item was a small T-shirt with the band's logo on the front and "Stephen's BIGGEST Fan" on the back.

"It's adorable," she exclaimed, leaning to hug him.

He held her until she pulled back. "Did you see Jonathan?"

"The nursery blinds were closed."

Genny sighed. "He's the most beautiful baby."

"You wouldn't be slightly prejudiced?"

"Maybe just a little," she agreed, stretching her arms wide to indicate how much.

Stephen chuckled. "Feel up to a ride to the hospital?"

She could think of nothing she wanted more, but it was a long trip. "It's too much trouble. You'd have to bring me back. Dr. Garner wants me to rest, but I can't think about anything but Jonathan. It's not fair."

He looked puzzled. "What's keeping you here?"

"Money. We are dependent on Sonya for everything."

"Why didn't you ask for my help?"

She looked him in the eye. "You've done so much."

"Let's go see Jonathan. And talk about this."

Genny looked down at the clothes she'd worn from the hospital. They were terribly wrinkled.

"Try the dress," he suggested. "Or is there something you'd rather wear?"

The meager contents of her wardrobe, including the shabby, secondhand collection that comprised her maternity wear, held nothing she cared to be seen in and nothing that would fit until her body returned to normal. Genny couldn't remember the last time she'd gone shopping. Sonya had bought the cheap maternity dresses, claiming she was sick of the robe Genny had lived in since the funeral.

"No, it would be a pleasure to wear something new."

Genny slipped into the bathroom and disposed of the wrinkled garment. A wave of dizziness hit when she slipped the dress over her head. She reached out, the palm of her hand hitting the door with a hollow thud.

"Genny?"

The door popped open, removing her prop. Stephen caught her. "Are you okay?"

"I overbalanced. Could you tie the sash for me?"

Genny's skin grew warmer as the vision of Stephen in the role of husband planted itself in her head. *Don't be ridiculous,* she admonished.

He helped her to the sofa. "Let me put the water container back in the refrigerator, and we'll go. Hope you don't mind. I was thirsty."

"Not at all. I should have asked. I'm a horrible hostess."

He seemed distracted when he returned. Eager to see Jonathan, Genny pushed her questions away. Seeing her son would put things in the proper light—remind her what was important.

five

She isn't coming back to this house until Jonathan is released from the hospital, Stephen decided as he helped Genny into his car. Accomplishing such a feat would take a miracle, but it had to be done.

Stephen felt guilty. He had not been completely honest with Genny. He'd flabbergasted everyone by walking out after the Texas concert. He hadn't been able to get Genny off his mind. Seeing her only reinforced his need to help.

He had no business nosing around, but a fridge stocked with nothing but ice water and condiments made him see red. Only Genny's bumping the door saved him from reacting angrily.

ॐ

"Something wrong?" Genny ventured only to receive a taciturn response. Bewildered, she rested her head against the seat and closed her eyes. First Sonya, now Stephen. No one ever seemed to have anything to say to her. What had happened? She'd been so glad to see him, almost frightened by the joy having him near brought.

He owed her nothing. She expected nothing. Loneliness made her so happy to see him. Soon she'd see Jonathan, talk to him, and just look until he fell asleep. She could hardly wait until they let her bring him home. He was hers to love, even if he couldn't talk or reassure her when the doubts were overwhelming.

"We're here."

She awoke to find they were at the hospital. When he opened the door, Genny moved quickly, dropping back with the wave of dizziness that swept over her.

Stephen kneeled before her, his hands warm as he chaffed

her cold fingers. "I'll get a doctor."

She caught hold of his arms. "I'm fine."

He looked doubtful at best. "This can't be good. I'm going to talk to your doctor."

Genny's agitation increased when Stephen blocked her way. "I'm sorry I frightened you, but I have to see Jonathan now."

❧

Just who am I angry with? Stephen wondered as he escorted Genny inside. *Sonya for having to work? John for dying? Myself for not being able to do more?* He'd already done more than most men would do for a virtual stranger. Why? Because it was no less than Jesus expected of him? Maybe, but he suspected a deeper-seated reason.

"What time do you finish? There are a couple of things I need to handle, but I'd like to take you to dinner."

"I usually stay for an hour."

His hand rested protectively at the small of her back. In the elevator, a teenage girl studied him. "You're Stephen Camden," she exclaimed.

She dug around in a minute purse and checked her coat pockets. At her regret-filled sigh, Genny produced a slip of paper, and he scribbled his name.

"You made her day," Genny said after the doors closed behind them. The full benefit of her grin took Stephen by surprise. "She seemed surprised when you got off on the maternity floor. Let's hope this doesn't turn into some sort of tabloid nightmare. 'Country Maverick Fathers Child' or something like that."

Stephen frowned. "I hate it when people consider me public property. Is it so impossible that I have friends with babies?"

"It can't be helped. The handsome young bachelor image doesn't hurt your star status."

Star status. He only wanted to perform his music. Stephen eyed the hand Genny laid on his arm before he looked into her face.

"I happen to think you're great with your fans."

"It's hard, Genny. They're always watching, waiting for me to make the headlines. I wish I could say I've become used to something as simple as taking a walk with a woman being turned into an overnight sensation, but I haven't."

"I wouldn't either," she admitted.

Their steps quickened as they neared the nursery. Stephen gestured toward the closed blinds. "How am I supposed to see my biggest fan?"

"I'll arrange it."

☙

Genny entered the door marked Hospital Personnel Only. Once inside, her gaze shifted to Jonathan's isolette, and her breath slipped out in a thankful sigh. She had worried terribly about leaving him.

She explained the situation to the head nurse, and the woman agreed to her plan. Genny stepped to the door and gestured Stephen inside.

He shook his head. "I'll look through the glass."

"If that's what you want," Genny said, unable to hide her disappointment.

"I don't want to intrude."

"You could never do that."

☙

Stephen shrugged and followed Genny to the scrub area.

A few minutes later, he found himself fighting back jealousy when she smiled at another man.

"How's she doing today?"

"The same," he said softly. "Coming here helps."

Genny nodded and whispered to Stephen, "His wife's in a coma."

He watched over her shoulder as Genny touched Jonathan through the portholes. Mesmerized by her soft tone, he found himself unable to look away. She sparkled, her expression proud as she sought his opinion.

"He's growing." His reward was a delighted grin.

"You really think so?"

Upon recognizing the hope in Genny's expression, he became more cautious. "The scales will tell." Jonathan's crying saved the moment. "Even sooner if I get out of here. Enjoy yourself."

"Stephen, wait," Genny called. "You didn't touch him."

"I don't—"

"He doesn't bite." Genny slid one hand along Jonathan's arm.

Stephen smiled at Jonathan's response to his mother. "Spoiled already."

"I think he recognizes my touch. Come on. Say hello."

Their shoulders brushed as he moved beside Genny and slid his hand into the lower porthole. She laughed when Jonathan extended his legs, and Stephen jerked his hand back.

"It's okay. The nurses tell me premature babies benefit from touching. Still think he's beautiful?"

His head snapped up, their gazes locking. Jonathan's skin might be as wrinkled as that of an old man, ruddy in color, and covered in a fine layer of hair, but Stephen couldn't shake the feeling that wrapped itself about his heart as his gaze moved from mother to son and back. He nodded.

"Me too." Her gaze moved to the baby.

"I'll be back," he said.

"Stephen," Genny called. He looked at her. "You don't have to come back. I mean. . . Well, I know you're busy. You probably have a million things to do after being away."

He stripped off the gown and stuffed it into the container. "What if I want to, Gen?"

"We'd love to see you."

&

She stretched her time with Jonathan as long as possible before relinquishing his care to the nurses. Genny slipped out the door and stood before the window comparing babies.

"Ready?"

Startled by Stephen's voice, she jumped. "Did you finish your errands?"

"They didn't take as long as I thought."

Stephen took her arm. The image of his hand landing as gently as a butterfly on a flower when he touched Jonathan came to her mind as they walked to his car.

"Where are we going?" she asked when he drove past the Nashville exit.

"My house. I asked Mrs. James to prepare dinner."

Stephen kept up a steady stream of conversation, urging Genny to talk about herself.

"Not fair. You already know everything about me."

He grinned. "I suppose I do have the advantage. Fear, or maybe pain, turns you into a talker."

"And what turns you into a talker?"

Genny found the answer was music as he said very little about himself and more about the band.

A large mailbox which appeared to have suffered from contact with someone's vehicle marked the turnoff. His house sat far off the road, down a winding driveway outlined with a white wooden fence.

Genny found the carefully renovated old brick home to be in stark contrast with the unlandscaped yard. Inside, the country place turned out to be her dream house. "Oh, Stephen, it's beautiful!" she cried, her head whirling as she tried to take it all in at once. All the trimmings, fireplaces, and French doors were improved rather than deleted.

"Thanks to my sister, Jane, the interior decorator. She relieved me of a chunk of my savings and convinced me it was the right thing. I am pleased with how it turned out. Only problem is I don't get to spend much time here."

Genny sighed. His beautiful home sat empty while she holed up in one bedroom at Sonya's condo. She supposed she should be thankful she had a roof over her head.

"Have a seat. I'll check on dinner."

Comfortable leather furniture had been grouped to take advantage of the gorgeous marble fireplace that served as the focal point of the living room.

"Ready to eat?" Stephen asked.

China, crystal, and gold flatware on a lace cloth gave the table a festive appearance. A huge, cut flower centerpiece adorned the table.

"Mrs. James prepared all my favorites," Stephen said as he seated her. "Hopefully, there's something on the menu you like."

Genny devoured every bite of the tender steak and fat baked potato dripping with butter, sour cream, and chives. "I was greedy."

"You were hungry," Stephen said.

She didn't deny the truth. Her meager lunch hadn't sustained her very long. "You're fortunate to have such a wonderful cook."

Stephen nodded. "Blessed. I tell her often. Let's go into the den."

She immediately recognized the den as "his" room. Stephen's stamp was everywhere. Packages covered the coffee table and floor. "You getting an early start on Christmas?"

"Would you believe me if I said yes?"

Genny noted the baby gift wrap and shook her head.

"Okay, it's an impromptu baby shower. The guys told their wives and girlfriends about Jonathan, and the next thing I knew, my house had become the depository. You can't send them back."

"Why would I want to?" Genny asked, her attention focused on a huge balloon filled with baby accessories.

"I thought maybe because the guys were strangers. . ."

Genny chuckled. "We became pretty intimate friends very quickly. And for the record, where my child is concerned, I have no pride. He needs things I can't afford to buy."

Confusion flashed across his face. "So why do you refuse my help?"

"Because you do too much."

"No more than I want to do. Is Sonya planning a shower?"

Genny shook her head. "She hates that sort of thing. Help

me open the presents. Save the names," she cautioned. "I have to write thank-you notes."

Like kids, they dove into the pile of presents. Stephen opted to strip away the paper and pass the gifts to Genny. An explosion garnered a tiny scream followed by laughter when a balloon fragment landed in her lap.

He shrugged. "I tried to figure out how to open it."

"They thought of everything. Even preemie outfits for him to wear when he's released."

Stephen watched her refold the tiny garments. "Genny, have you ever thought God brought us together for a reason?"

Her gaze touched on him and then moved to the box she held. "I think God's deserted me."

"Losing your husband and having a premature child has been difficult, but God hasn't left you."

"Why wouldn't I think that, Stephen? All my life, I've tried to be good and look where it's gotten me. I'm a thirty-six-year-old mother with no way to support her child and no home for him when he leaves the hospital. I'm not even sure how much of the medical bills will be paid."

❧

Stephen prayed for answers. No doubt Christians suffered and most of the time their suffering turned them back to God. His own suffering enabled him to comfort others, but he believed all the praise and glory belonged to God. His belief assured him one day he would leave the worries of the world behind.

"I'm sorry. I shouldn't have said that," Genny said. "Everything seems so hopeless."

"What happened to your home?"

"Sonya sold it. No, it's not like that," Genny said at his surprised look. "I couldn't have survived without her help. After John died, I barely functioned. The house had to be sold to pay the debts."

What kind of help? Stephen wondered. "What about John's life insurance?"

"There wasn't any. I do try to thank God, and you've given me even more reason to be appreciative. Oh, look at this!" Genny cried, pulling the clown puppet over her hand and thumbing through the accompanying storybook. "I read to Jonathan before he was born."

"So what else do you like besides reading?"

"Cooking, decorating, and I adore gardening. I miss my yard more than my house. I couldn't keep my gorgeous plants when I moved to Sonya's."

"There's a greenhouse out back. I like to tinker there when I have time."

"What do you grow?" Genny asked, clearly excited that they shared a love of gardening.

"Not much of anything lately," Stephen said, smiling grimly. "I miss puttering around, getting my hands dirty. I grew the violets in the dining room."

"Ooh, they're my favorites," she exclaimed. "So delicate."

"And hard to grow. I love a challenge."

The discussion drifted on to other plant preferences, and Genny listened intently as Stephen outlined his plan to land-scape his yard.

"I'll probably end up hiring someone to do the work. Genny, I've been thinking. . . . I'd like to make you an offer. For Jonathan's sake. You can say no if you want, but please think about it first." She nodded. "I'd like for you to use my guest-house." He expected a refusal based solely on her expression.

"Stephen, you've done far too much already."

"Let me show you the place. Then consider the convenience factor. You're going to be miserable away from Jonathan."

"But I can't pay you," she protested.

"And I'm not asking you to. Let me get the key."

❧

Stunned, Genny stared after Stephen when he charged from the room. He couldn't know how much she appreciated the gifts. They'd provided every item she'd anguished over. And now Stephen wanted to provide her with a place to stay.

"Let's go take a look," he said, dangling the key ring from his finger.

They went through French doors into a garden badly in need of care.

"Sorry about this eyesore. The landscapers want me to work with them, and there's never time."

"It has great potential," Genny said, thinking of the tiny yard she'd turned into a beautiful garden. She had done all the designing and implementing herself, buying every bulb, plant, and tree in the area. She'd enjoyed every moment. Receiving the local gardening club's monthly award several times was just icing on the cake.

They approached a smaller version of the big house. In the distance, Genny could see other buildings. "Do you have acreage here?"

"About fifty." Stephen opened the door and flipped on the light. "This is the place I had in mind for you."

It was one large room, subtly divided into three areas—kitchen, bedroom, and sitting room. Her gaze was drawn to the small fireplace flanked by single French doors. "It's beautiful," Genny said.

"And if Jonathan gets released from the hospital but needs to stay in the area, you could use this room as a nursery," Stephen said, showing her a dressing room large enough for the baby's crib and furnishings, including a rocker. "You could leave the door open at night."

He's given this more than a little thought, Genny realized. "We don't need anything half as grand."

"It's here and it's empty. Don't say no when you really want to say yes so badly."

He spoke the truth. The few hours had seemed an eternity. How would she survive several days without seeing her son? And even then, she'd have to listen to Sonya's complaints about the toll calls to the hospital and the expense of Genny commuting to and from the hospital. It would be so reassuring to have Stephen so close—when he wasn't on the road.

Genny smiled at him. "I'll think about it. I promise. I do appreciate the offer and everything you've done for us."

He nodded. "We'd better get you home. I'm sure you've done more today than the doctor wanted."

She touched his arm. "I will consider your offer, Stephen."

"That's all I ask. I'm praying you'll make the right decision."

six

They returned to find Mrs. James had boxed and bagged all the gifts, and minutes later they were in the car headed to Nashville. The conversation was casual, comfortable, nothing like the tongue-tied efforts Genny expected.

She waited for Stephen to prod her into accepting his offer, but he said nothing. The urge to say yes was overwhelming, but she couldn't keep taking. While Sonya believed there was nothing wrong with taking advantage of things freely given, Genny disagreed. Taking advantage of people was wrong. Then again, she didn't think Stephen felt she was using him.

Back at the condo, Stephen carried the packages in. "I suppose you're sleeping on the sofa?"

"No stairs."

"What if I carried you up? You'd probably enjoy a shower."

Genny shook her head. "Then you'd have to come back tomorrow and bring me down and. . ."

"I've done too much already."

She touched his arm. "Don't be upset."

He stepped closer, watching her. "Think about my offer?"

"I am," Genny said. "You're much too generous, Stephen."

"I won't let you down."

His comment puzzled her. "You don't owe me anything."

"Pray about this, Genny. Don't make yourself miserable when there's no reason."

His earnestness touched her heart. She wanted Jonathan in his bassinet by her bed, not hours away. Genny nodded agreement, fighting back the tears that sprang to her eyes.

"I'm sorry. I shouldn't have reminded you," Stephen said. "How about a hug?"

Genny wrapped her arms about him and appreciated his

46

comforting touch. She smiled at his admonition not to worry. The soft kiss caught her by surprise, but she didn't pull away.

"I'll tell the guys you love the baby stuff."

She stepped back. "Please do. I need their addresses. I'd like to send personal notes."

Stephen pulled out his wallet and thumbed through the cards. "Contact this office and tell them I gave you the number. They can help."

"You think they'll believe me?"

"Probably not." He turned the card over and jotted an address. "Send them to me. I'll see they're delivered."

"Thanks, Stephen."

"And here's my number. So you can reach me. Don't hesitate to call."

Genny's throat constricted and her eyes watered.

"Mrs. James says you need to gain weight. She put a few things in this basket. I'll stick them in the refrigerator."

She sighed. Any minute now, he'd probably give her his wallet and the shirt off his back. "I told you Sonya would take care of that."

He paused and looked at her. "Where is she, Genny?"

"At work."

"At ten o'clock at night?" His gray eyes sparkled like a flash of lightning in a summer thunderstorm. "Has she even called to check on you?"

Genny met his ravings with defense of her sister. "Sonya hoped to get home around six. It's a busy time for her. She said so when she brought me home today."

"And left you here. Did she even bother to check to see if there was anything for you to eat?"

"She didn't have time."

"Don't defend her," he snapped. "I saw the contents of your refrigerator. What time would you have eaten? Midnight? Tomorrow? No doubt you're having dizzy spells. You've got to be sensible, Genny, or you'll be back in the hospital. Maybe you should be anyway."

Her ire increased with his misunderstanding of the situation. "I'm doing the best I can."

She couldn't criticize Sonya. Not unless she wanted to risk making herself and her son homeless. "I have no money. What Sonya does for me out of the kindness of her heart is all I can expect."

His lips twisted in a cynical smile. "She doesn't have a heart."

Genny turned away.

Stephen touched her shoulder. His tone thawed. "I don't want to argue. I can't bear to think of you in this situation."

She stared deep into his eyes, seeing the things she'd imagined in her daydreams of him. Friendship had quickly turned into attraction on her part. His voice could soothe and excite at the same time. His presence reassured and pleased.

"Ever since I laid eyes on you, I've wanted to be with you. I think about you a thousand times a day, wondering how you and Jonathan are doing. The phone calls aren't enough."

Genny stared down at the floor.

"I'm sorry," Stephen whispered, cradling her chin with his fingertips.

"Sonya tries, Stephen. But she has a busy life."

"And I can't help but believe you need someone to look after you."

"I can take care of myself."

"Under ordinary circumstances, but there's nothing ordinary here. You don't have other relatives who can help?"

Genny shook her head, more tears coming to her eyes as she considered her solitude in the world.

"We'll find a way," Stephen said, pulling her into his arms.

She rested against his chest, feeling secure and safer than she had in quite some time.

He cupped her chin and pulled her face up to his.

She reacted in fear, wrenching herself from his arms. "No. Don't."

"Genny, don't run away."

"There's nothing about me that is even remotely like the

women you associate with."

"Maybe that's why." He massaged the hand that rested between his larger ones. "There's never been a right woman for me. I think you could be."

"Don't be ridiculous. We shared something special. That memory is what you can't erase from your head."

"That memory has your face, your voice. Do you want me out of your life?"

Genny felt the stirrings of something more powerful than either of them but knew she couldn't take the risk. "We can't base a relationship on a memory."

"But we could base it on a friendship," Stephen said. He invaded her space again, and Genny didn't move away.

"Oh, Stephen, I don't know."

"What is it, Genny? Is it that you're not ready?"

Her legs threatened to give away. If only she could explain her confusion. The way things had been with her husband. . . her fears that she had been losing John before the baby. . .

"It's me," Genny admitted without further explanation, intent on escaping Stephen. She had to think. She couldn't explain. For the past months her life had run out of control. She'd be a fool to hope she could ever have anything with a man like Stephen Camden.

His world was as far from her own as the earth from the moon. But unlike the astronauts, she lacked the ability to explore new worlds. Her own, such as it was, had to be enough.

"Stephen," she whispered, reaching out to him.

"I don't want apologies."

"I don't want to hurt. . . ," she stuttered, staring deep into gray eyes that burned with emotion.

"Get some rest."

After he left, Genny sank down on the couch. Stephen wasn't fooled by her halfhearted refusals. He knew exactly what she needed. And although she knew she should be telling him no, Genny couldn't turn him away. She needed his caring—desperately.

Like other women, she'd appreciated Stephen Camden from afar. Now she knew a different side of the handsome singer, the real man.

Genny lifted her legs onto the sofa and covered them with the blanket. She would rest for a few minutes. The door opening woke her.

"What time is it?" she asked.

"Late," Sonya said. "Why is the lamp on?"

"I dozed off."

She flipped the switch, leaving the room in darkness. "Turn off the lights next time. Electricity is expensive."

"Sonya, do you have a minute? There's something I'd like to discuss with you."

"Can't it wait?" The sigh Sonya had perfected echoed in the room. "I suppose you'll obsess all night if I don't hear you out."

"I just wondered if there was something I could do at your office to earn some money."

"Do you honestly think I'd put my job on the line by recommending you?" Sonya scoffed.

"I want to support myself."

Sonya's sarcastic laugh filled the dark void. "The best you can hope for is minimum wage. That would hardly keep the baby in diapers, much less day care. You can't afford to work."

"It'll be a struggle, but I need a job."

A case snapped open, and the glow of the lighter lit Sonya's face. A red pinpoint light glowed, and the odor of tobacco smoke dominated the room. "You have no idea what a real struggle is."

Don't I? A real struggle was holding your temper in check while your only relative accused you of living in a fantasy world. Where was the fantasy? She was a woman with a child and no money, no prospects for a job, and definitely no supportive relatives.

She'd placed her faith in her husband, expecting him to provide for their future. Instead he had taken that future to the grave with him, leaving her impoverished and plagued with worry. For the first time in her life, Genny didn't know how to overcome adversity.

If she had to be dependent on the kindness of others, chances were she would be better off depending on someone who knew the meaning of the word. "Stephen offered me use of his guesthouse while Jonathan is in the hospital. I think maybe I'll take him up on his offer."

"What makes every man you come in contact with feel duty bound to protect you?"

"They don't," Genny objected.

"Hah. It can't be because you're a raving beauty." The light flashed on. Sonya hunted an ashtray and stubbed out the cigarette. "You say he offered you his guesthouse? When?"

"Tonight. He came to visit and took me to see Jonathan. Afterward, we went to his house for dinner."

"Just who is this guy?"

"Stephen Camden. He's the lead singer for Cowboy Jamboree."

Sonya's head snapped up. "You're kidding."

"Stephen rescued me when I went into labor. He's been a great friend."

"Why didn't you tell me this before?"

"You haven't exactly wanted to hear the story, Sonya."

"This is fantastic."

Genny recognized Sonya's enthusiasm for what it was. "I won't take advantage of his kindness."

"You owe me."

What about everything she and John had done for Sonya? Why was it their kindness account always seemed to be in the debit column? In the year before his death, John had spent more time doing chores for her sister than for her.

"I've pulled my weight around here, Sonya. I cleaned your house, did your laundry, shopped for food, and cooked meals when you could be bothered to come home to eat them."

"It's not taking advantage," Sonya cajoled, changing her tone. "We're family, sisters helping each other. All I want to do is drop by, get to know him a little better, and then sell him on my firm. Is that too much to ask?"

"It's not your firm," Genny argued. "You're a secretary. You can't sell anything."

"I don't plan to be a secretary forever," Sonya all but shouted. "I have my savings, and if I could lure a big group to the firm, I'd be on the fast track to the top."

"He's offered me his guesthouse."

"This solves a problem for you, doesn't it? Just remember that when the fantasy days are over and you come back to the real world, it's going to take a better-paying job to support the three of us. It would be smart if you helped me now so I could help you later. I'm going to bed."

Sonya moved up the stairs without saying good night.

Don't lose hope. You won't be a burden forever. Genny recited these words in her head. Sonya would see. She would find a means of supporting herself and Jonathan. As soon as the doctor released her and Jonathan was out of the hospital, she'd show Sonya just how well-grounded her world really was.

Genny stumbled to the bathroom in the dark, her heart stinging from Sonya's repeated put-downs. Tears streamed down her cheeks as she considered her financial situation. How could John have left them with nothing? They had discussed investments. She knew he'd made them. Had he lost the money and been too ashamed to tell her the truth?

One step at a time. For now, she needed to get her son out of the hospital. Then she would find a means of providing their own home. If it meant living in a studio apartment, she'd do that rather than feel like a burden to anyone.

At least she wasn't in debt. She'd paid all the funeral expenses, outstanding bills, and continued the health insurance premiums, which would pay a portion of Jonathan's astronomical medical bills. She and the baby weren't totally destitute—at least they had John's Social Security benefits.

Maybe she didn't have much more than her pride and her child, but they were enough.

seven

Genny's agony increased overnight. Her longing to be with Jonathan overwhelmed her.

When the phone rang the following morning, she grabbed the kitchen extension. Genny experienced a fresh flow of tears at the sound of Stephen's voice.

"Gen? What's wrong?"

"It's. . . ," she began shakily, growing quiet as she fought for control. "Nothing," she managed finally. She did not sound the least convincing.

"Honey, tell me."

Genny wavered before she said, "Oh, Stephen, everything's awful. What am I going to do?"

"Has something happened? Is Jonathan okay?"

"Sonya and I talked about me getting a job. She says I can't earn enough to keep my son in diapers." A mighty sniff followed the words. "Why does she have to be so cruel?"

"Why are you worrying about this now?" he demanded. "You need to recover before you start thinking about the future."

Genny knew Stephen would never understand her need for independence until he fully understood the position she'd placed herself in. "I shouldn't be burdening you with my problems. I'm an awful imposition on your good nature."

"You never could be," he assured. "How's Jonathan?"

Genny went into raptures over her son, describing the little things the nurses had shared, laughing with Stephen as he teased her into a good humor once more.

"What if I pick you up and take you to the hospital? Would you like that?"

"Yes," Genny said. "Yes, I would. And Stephen," she began,

finding the words hard to express, "if the offer is still open, I'd like to stay in your guesthouse for a couple of weeks. I can't bear not seeing Jonathan. It's like a part of me is lying in that nursery."

"The place is yours for as long as you need it. Now stop worrying. I'll help with your things when I get there."

"I'll be ready."

"Remember, no stairs," he cautioned.

"Okay," Genny said, hating the feeling of helplessness.

She replaced the receiver, finding herself in deep thought when Sonya came into the kitchen wearing an expensive, red power suit. Her sister's executive wardrobe went far beyond that of most secretaries.

"Who was on the phone?"

"Stephen. He's picking me up today."

"To visit the baby?"

Genny concentrated on pouring juice. "I'm moving into his guesthouse for two weeks."

"That's my girl," Sonya praised, her face breaking into a smile. "Let me know a good time to visit, and we'll have him eating out of our hands in no time."

Determination filled Genny. "I won't let you hurt him."

Sonya frowned and exclaimed, "Why would I want to hurt Stephen Camden?"

Because I know you. Sonya used people to achieve her goals. "You're my sister and I don't think Stephen would mind you visiting, but I'm not getting involved in your schemes."

"That's my job," Sonya said, radiating confidence. "And what a coup it will be." She all but danced out the door.

No doubt Sonya was certain she could do anything she set her mind to. In the looks department, her sibling netted everything Genny missed out on. Gorgeous blond hair, now twisted into a professional style for work, hung down her back in a golden waterfall when she released the constraints. Large blue eyes tempted men to look into her very soul. There were absolutely no comparisons between Sonya's curvaceous body and Genny's sparse frame. People always expressed disbelief that they were sisters.

The ones who bothered to look beyond the beautiful exterior generally got a good glimpse of Sonya's self-centeredness. No man had ever withstood Sonya's need to be the star of the relationship.

Now it was her job to ensure that Stephen didn't fall prey to Sonya's games. Her vow not to see him hurt was far more important to Genny than Sonya's lofty goals.

Genny spent the wait sorting through the mess in the living room, folding blankets, and repacking the small suitcase. She felt tempted to climb the stairs. She could pack and be downstairs before Stephen arrived. Maybe he'd think Sonya had packed her clothes. One foot touched the bottom tread just as the doorbell rang.

Feeling guilty, Genny opened the door and met his smile with one of her own. "You made the trip in record time."

He hugged her. "I've always had a heavy foot. Feeling better?"

Genny nodded, unable to get the words around the emotion clogging her throat.

"Let's get you packed. Mrs. James is airing the guesthouse and making the bed. Don't be surprised if she plans a special dinner by way of welcome."

"Stephen, please don't go out of your way. Letting me stay in the guesthouse is far too much."

He grinned and swung her up into his arms. "Nothing's too much for my friends," he insisted as they reached the landing. "Which room is yours?"

Genny indicated the smaller bedroom as he lowered her to her feet. His gaze moved about the tiny, furniture-packed space.

"It's crowded. These were the pieces I had to keep when I moved out of my house," Genny explained, attempting to shift the rocker so she could open the closet door.

"Do you want to take all of it to the guesthouse?"

"Oh no," Genny said. "Not for two weeks."

"Why do you insist on two weeks?" Stephen demanded, moving the chair out of the way. "You have no idea how long Jonathan will be in the hospital."

He had no way of knowing how she felt about being dependent on others. "I'm hoping."

"Let's agree to play this by ear. Where's your suitcase?"

Stephen dragged the largest suitcase from the closet and laid it open on the bed. Genny slid her limited wardrobe along the closet railing. Only a couple of pieces were decent enough to be seen in public. She laid them over the back of the rocker and walked over to the dresser.

"Stephen, there's a robe on the back of the bathroom door. Would you get it for me?"

He returned with the faded terry cloth garment.

"On second thought. . . ," Genny said as she examined the tattered sash.

"Looks fine to me. I have this shirt the guys keep threatening to burn. I keep it hidden when I don't have it on."

He wasn't wearing the shirt today. Stephen looked very handsome in khaki slacks and a leather jacket over a button-down collar shirt.

Resigned, Genny folded the robe and tucked in into the case. It was the only one she had.

∾

As he watched, Stephen wondered how any woman survived with so few clothes. Granted, she didn't strike him as the most fashion-conscious woman around, but she needed more than a couple of changes of clothes.

"That should do it."

There was still room in the suitcase.

"What about Jonathan's clothes?"

"I should take a few things. Just in case."

Stephen left Genny packing her cosmetic items as he carried the suitcase to the car. *I take more stuff than this on a two-day tour,* he thought incredulously as he lifted it into the trunk.

Back inside, he ran up the stairs. "Okay, what else?"

"Just this." Genny held up a plastic shopping bag filled with her personal items.

"Okay, let's go." Stephen swung her up into his arms and descended the stairs. She wasn't much heavier than her luggage. "Where's your coat?" he asked, releasing his hold on her.

Genny indicated the heavy sweater. "I'd like to take the gifts. Let me get my purse, and I'm ready."

"You don't have anything heavier? It's cold out there."

"I'm not much of a coat person. The sweater's warm."

Probably because she doesn't own a coat, Stephen thought. "Okay, I'll put this in the car and start up the heater while you finish in here."

He started out the door, pausing when she called his name. "Is it okay if I leave your address and phone number for Sonya?"

Even though he wanted to separate Genny from her sister's hurtful ways, he knew he couldn't refuse. "Sure."

"Oh, I need the thank-you notes. They're upstairs in my nightstand."

"Top drawer?"

"Yes. The flowered box."

Stephen pulled the drawer open and hesitated at the stack of photographs of Genny's dead husband staring up at him. "Hey, buddy, hope it's okay that I'm taking care of her for you," he whispered softly. The still photograph offered no clues.

"Okay, got them," he called down to Genny. "Do you want his photograph on the nightstand?"

"No, thanks."

She probably has a wallet-sized one, he thought. Stephen shrugged and made his way downstairs. He tucked the box in the bag. "Ready?"

Genny nodded and checked one last time to make certain she had the door key. "I always feel I've forgotten something."

"We can replace anything. I imagine the hospital is number one on your priority list?"

Genny smiled. "Only slightly ahead of thanking you."

❧

The trip seemed to take forever. After he parked, Genny all but floated to the nursery where the nurses welcomed her with smiles. They stayed a couple of hours before Stephen said, "I think maybe it's time for you to take a nap too."

"Just a couple minutes more," Genny said, caressing Jonathan's leg. "I missed him so much yesterday."

"He's a precious gift from heaven," Stephen agreed. "I'll wait for you in the lobby."

Genny thought about Stephen's words as she looked at her son. She did thank God for Jonathan's survival, but that didn't stop her from wondering why her tiny babe had to endure this.

Her life had never been perfect, but she tried to be a good person. Maybe it was time to look deeper. Suddenly Genny felt very tired. Stephen was right. She needed rest.

Stephen told her to pay attention to the route they took to his house. "You can drive this car to the hospital."

"Stephen! No!"

"Why not?" His expression resembled that of a disappointed child. "How did you plan to get there?"

"You've done much too much already."

"I'd like to do more," he said simply.

Leaning on Stephen Camden could easily become a habit. She couldn't let him get caught up in taking care of her. "I appreciate the offer, but I can get a taxi."

"Taxis are expensive."

"I'll go in the morning and spend the day."

Stephen shook his head. "You can't. The doctor doesn't want you at the hospital all the time."

"It's my problem. I'll work it out."

Genny tensed at his dissatisfied snort. "It isn't like you're putting me out. I won't be using the car. Wouldn't it be nice to drive yourself?"

"Dr. Garner doesn't want me driving."

"That's right," Stephen said. "Some of the guys said their wives couldn't drive right after the baby was born. Besides,

ith those dizzy spells, it probably isn't a good idea for you
o be behind the wheel yet. At least let me arrange your
ansportation."

Genny shook her head in disbelief. "You're a stubborn,
ubborn man."

"I like doing things for my friends."

"Well, this friend likes doing things for herself."

"But, Genny. . ."

"No, Stephen. I have to provide for my son."

He frowned. "I didn't realize you were so stubborn."

"I don't consider taking charge of my life as being stubborn."

꩜

tephen parked and went around to Genny's side to help her
ut. "Let's get you inside. I'll get your stuff."

"Stop treating me like fragile china. I had a baby, not major
rgery."

"I only want to help. It's cold out here, and that sweater is
ot all that thick," he protested.

"Fine. I'll sit on the couch like a good little girl. But you're
nly bringing my things inside, not unpacking or having
em unpacked."

He threw his hands into the air and backed off. "Okay.
Iere's your key to the guesthouse. Let yourself in. I'll bring
ne luggage and get out of your hair."

"Stephen, I'm sorry," Genny said softly. "I don't mean to
ound ungrateful, but you've got to let me do some things for
yself."

Take it easy, Man, he cautioned. "I'm sorry too. Mrs. James
an bring your dinner out here."

"I'll come over for dinner. If you don't mind," she said
entatively.

He nodded. Stephen placed her things in the bedroom
rea, told her to get some rest, and left. At home, he shut the
oor with a bit more force than necessary. Why wouldn't she
et him take care of her? He didn't want to take over her
fe—just arrange transportation to the hospital.

She wasn't going to sit in the hospital waiting room all day. And she wasn't going to catch a bus or a cab. He picked up the phone and punched in the number.

"I need the name of the limo service we use here in town."

"Certainly, Mr. Camden. I'll get it for you."

The band's newest release came over the phone as she put him on hold.

"Steve, Man, what's up? You trying to impress some chick?"

Stephen groaned when Chuck's voice came over the phone. "Just making arrangements for a friend."

"Female, I bet. Anyone I know?"

"It's none of your business, Harper."

"Awfully protective, aren't you?"

Stephen's head filled with Chuck Harper's exploits to publicize the band. He wouldn't let him number Genny among that group. "It's people like you she needs protection from."

"I'm only doing my job."

"If you want to keep that job, you'll remember what I said."

☙

Genny did a double take the following morning when she opened the door to the uniformed chauffeur intent on driving her to the hospital in a black stretch limousine.

"There must be some mistake."

"No, Ma'am. I'm Karen. Mr. Camden said to give you this."

She unfolded the paper and was struck by the bold slant of writing. *Genny,* she read, wondering if he had written the note or had told someone what to write.

> *I know what you said but the limo company has been instructed to take you to and from the hospital every day until Jonathan comes home. Please understand and do this for me. We'll be away for a few days. I'll call you soon.*
>
> *Stephen*

"I just started working with my dad today," the young woman said when Genny hesitated. "You wouldn't make me go back and tell him my first client refused to ride with me, would you?"

Genny smiled and shook her head. "Let me get my purse."

What was Stephen thinking? She rushed around gathering her things. She locked the door and walked over to where Karen waited by the open car door. Feeling like royalty, Genny climbed inside.

"Just relax and leave everything to me, Mrs. Smith. There's fruit juice in the refrigerator. Mr. Camden thought you might prefer that."

The rich smell of expensive leather filled her nose as Genny wallowed in the luxurious seat. "Oh, Stephen, what have you done?" she whispered.

"Did you say something, Ma'am?"

Genny waved her off. The door closed, secluding her in privacy, and she explored the area. Every nook and cranny held a surprise. She marveled at the telephone, television, and other conveniences she'd never thought to see in a vehicle— especially the chilled crystal goblets in the refrigerator!

Several taxis a day wouldn't cost this much. She would tell him so the next opportunity she had.

eight

Several days later, Genny lounged in the back of limo as if she'd been riding in them forever. Having transportation to and from the hospital was heavenly. Jonathan gained weight, and Dr. Lee felt encouraged. Genny shared the news with Stephen when he called, as he had done each night.

The first time, Genny confronted him about the limo. "I know you wanted to arrange transportation, but I never dreamed you'd go this far."

"It doesn't cost that much."

"Yeah, sure."

"No, really, these companies give us a good deal."

Genny wasn't convinced. "I don't know how I'll ever repay you."

"No need. I subscribe to the Second Corinthians 9:7 Scripture."

"What's that?" she asked curiously.

"The Bible reads, 'Each man should give what he has decided in his heart to give, not reluctantly or under compulsion, for God loves a cheerful giver.'

"Genny, one day, when you're able, you'll help someone in need. Meanwhile, get your strength back and bring Jonathan home so I can visit him without having to put my hands through portholes. I have nightmares about getting my hands stuck." With her laughter, he asked, "Can you do that for me?"

"Oh, Stephen," she whispered softly so he wouldn't hear, then answered, "Yes."

Genny concentrated on achieving the goal, following her doctor's advice to the letter and recovering from her pregnancy with no complications. Happiness coursed through her, particularly after spending time with her baby or talking with Stephen.

Sonya's question stayed on her mind, and Genny found she couldn't explain why men saw her as a little girl lost.

Genny never considered herself even remotely pretty. She was plain, a fact that made itself evident every time she looked into a mirror.

Granted, her mousy brown hair did have an attractive shine after a wash. But her face was a combination of sharp planes and angles, its shape a long thin heart with high cheeks and a sharp nose. She was short, with no physical allure. Her thin body had already thrust off the extra pregnancy weight, leaving no indication that she'd had a child. Forest green eyes were her only claim to beauty.

Guilt soared through her when she missed Stephen. She had no business thinking of another man so soon after John's death.

Still she felt delight when Stephen surprised her with an early morning visit. Feeling self-conscious in the tattered robe and looking less than her best, Genny invited him in. Her heart went out to him. He looked exhausted. "Would you like a cup of coffee?"

He nodded. Stephen sat on a stool, watching as she measured coffee into the coffee maker.

"Have you eaten?"

"We just got in."

She removed eggs and butter from the refrigerator and a frying pan from the cabinet. "How was the trip?"

"Hectic. Five cities in five days. Not to mention the recording session before that."

"When do you leave again?"

Stephen shrugged and yawned widely. "I don't even want to think about it."

"After breakfast, you need to go home and get some rest."

"Trying to get rid of me already?"

Genny nearly missed the teasing glint in his eye. "No!" she

cried. "I'd love for you to stay, but you need sleep."

"I know. I wanted to let you know I was back and ask if I can take you to the hospital later."

"I'd like that."

After Stephen went home to rest, Genny dressed for her trip to the hospital. Karen arrived right on schedule.

Climbing inside, she greeted her new friend and said, "Stephen's home. He'll drive me to the hospital this afternoon."

The realization that her two weeks was half over marred her visit. Stephen would never hold her to the self-imposed deadline, but she felt obligated to honor her original plan.

It would be different if she were able to return the favor. Even at Sonya's she'd held on to her pride by keeping house.

"Oh, Jonathan," she whispered to the sleeping baby, "why do things have to be this way?"

Genny expected no answer. As the parent, the adult, she had the responsibility of seeing that this child had a good life. She would find a way, and until then, she would depend on the kindness of others to see them through.

"Hello, Genny."

She jumped, reaching to erase the trace of tears from her cheeks. "Dr. Lee. Hello."

"How's our boy doing today?"

"You tell me."

"I'm happy to say he's improving daily."

Genny waited while the doctor checked over Jonathan's chart and then spoke to the nurses. "Dr. Lee, do you have a minute?" she asked when he started out the door.

"Certainly."

"Do you. . . ? I mean, I know you can't really. . ." Just spit it out. "I need to know how long Jonathan will be in the hospital."

He shook his head. "In cases like this, it's day to day. Jonathan is developing, in this particular case outside the uterus, much as he would have done inside your body. He needs to mature and gain weight before I would even consider releasing him. What troubles you, Genny?"

"I've been staying with a friend here in Memphis," she explained. "I limited my stay to two weeks. I hoped. . ."

"No, we're looking at much longer. Would your friend object to extending your visit?"

"I can't intrude indefinitely."

"You certainly have a dilemma, one you need to work out as quickly as possible. Stressed mothers make irritable babies."

"So would it be better for me to go home and wait for his release?"

"No! Never!" Dr. Lee insisted. "What's best is that you're here with him. And that you find peace within yourself. Talk to your friend. You might be surprised by his response."

The doctor's words surprised her. How had he known her friend was a man? Had Stephen been in contact with the doctor? Surely not. Then again, she'd told the nurses they could update him on Jonathan's status.

Dr. Lee was right about the need to find peace within herself.

Stephen joined her for the second visit, and afterward insisted Genny stay for dinner. Preoccupied, she enjoyed yet another tasty meal and found herself ready to beat a hasty retreat. Coward, she chastised as she wished him good night.

"Don't be in such a hurry," he said. "Come with me. I want you to hear something I'm working on."

Genny followed Stephen into his den. Piles of sheet music hung over the edge of coffee table. His guitar leaned against the sofa.

"You've been writing? I thought you'd be too exhausted."

"Yeah. I felt inspired when I woke."

Genny reached for one of the pages and stopped. "May I?" He nodded. She read through the lyrics, surprised to find it was a Christmas hymn. "Is this song for the band?"

"We're planning a Christmas album."

"This is beautiful. When will it be recorded?"

"We worked on it some before the tour. I wanted to get the album out last year, but it didn't happen." He reached for his guitar and strummed a few cords.

Genny felt goose bumps rise on her arms as he sang the song. As always, the story of her Savior's birth moved her. The idea that God could love one so unworthy always amazed her.

"I already promised the guys we'll be home for Christmas this year. Harper isn't real happy."

Genny saw more in his expression than in the words he spoke. "What's wrong, Stephen?"

His sigh was heavy and burdensome. "I want to leave the band."

"Then do it." Genny lifted a hand to her mouth.

A tight smile flitted across his face. "I wish it were that simple."

"Why does it have to be difficult?"

"How do I throw away the security? My band members have families. I can't take away their livelihood. And it could mean I wouldn't have money to support myself or a family when the time comes. I feel like such a weak Christian."

"God provides, Stephen. I'm living proof of that. Where would I be if not for winning the ticket that brought you into my life? Would my son be alive if you hadn't taken us into your care? I don't see any reason why you can't sing the songs you dream of doing. Artists cross over all the time. You could too."

A slow smile creased his face. "You make me believe it's possible."

"God saw fit to give you talent, and life's too short not to do what you want."

"I've been working on the other music when I'm home. The guys look at me strangely when I mention I've been putting in a lot of writing time because I haven't produced much in the way of music for the band."

"They haven't seen these?"

"No. Harper's been on my case to write more songs, but my heart's not in it."

"Figure out how to make it work."

Stephen leaned back against the sofa. "What's happened to

my faith that God will provide? I hate this power money has over my life. Years ago, before Christ came into my life, I loved the lifestyle. Now I despise everything about it. The concerts are okay but the drinking, profanity, and fighting in some of the small clubs overwhelm me. I want to stand on that stage and preach brotherly love, but I know they'd stone me if I tried. I know I should do it anyway," he admitted with a sigh.

"I jumped at the chance to do the Christmas hymns album. I'm more excited about this project than anything in a long while. Including the CMA Award."

"Sounds like you know what you want."

"I want to use my talent for God. I want my music to touch lives and share God's story."

"Then trust Him to make it possible."

Spouting off encouraging words of faith when in doubt herself made Genny feel like such a hypocrite.

"I know not to depend on myself, but humans are such strange creatures. We pray for guidance but more often than not wouldn't recognize the answer if it hit us over the head. I'm praying about this. Will you pray too?"

Would God even hear her prayers after so long? Genny nodded.

"What did Dr. Lee say about Jonathan today?"

"That he has no idea when they'll release him."

"Hallelujah. You're the answer to a prayer," he exclaimed. "Mrs. James is going on vacation, and I need a house sitter. You can stay, and I'll pay you."

Genny couldn't help but be suspicious.

"I know what you're thinking," Stephen said. "Sometimes I wonder why I bought a house. I never get to spend much time here. It would be a great help if you could stay. You can use my car. Mrs. James uses the car," Stephen said before she could object.

Genny gave up. "Okay. I won't fight you. I'll house-sit in exchange for the guesthouse and use of your car. I think I'm getting the better end of the deal."

"You obviously don't know how difficult it is to find house sitters. Even with the security system and such, I dread thinking of what would happen if I left the place empty."

No doubt the looters would steal him blind. "What about while I'm at the hospital?"

Stephen covered the wide yawn with his hand. "I'm more concerned about the house sitting empty."

"I'll take good care of your home."

"I don't doubt it." He yawned again.

"You're exhausted," Genny said.

"Let's just say I don't think I'll have any problems getting to sleep."

⸙

Stephen insisted on seeing Genny to the guesthouse and returned home to toss and turn in his bed, his need for sleep overcome by the guilt feelings.

He'd given Mrs. James two extra weeks of vacation, and knowing he only wanted to help Genny, she'd accepted. At least now he could relax a bit.

The earlier conversation with Genny troubled Stephen. Was he thwarting his own desire to serve the Lord in song? It certainly seemed that way. He closed his eyes and prayed, "Blessed Father, I realize I'm fighting You for control of my life. Help me to release my worries into Your hands and guide me to accept and achieve Your plan for me. Bless Genny and baby Jonathan. Thank You for bringing them into my life. Amen."

nine

The days passed, some quickly, and some as though they would never end. Genny felt even more confused. No matter how often she told herself guys like Stephen didn't fall for women like her, she couldn't forget her reaction to his presence. He filled her heart and soul, bringing more guilt when memories of John began to fade.

The battle of wills, Genny's attempts to curb Stephen's generosity overridden by his determination, seemed hopeless at times.

As planned, she reviewed the procedures of Stephen's house with Mrs. James before driving her to the airport. Every day, Genny checked the house, watered plants, dusted, and waited for Stephen's late-afternoon phone calls.

She looked forward to hearing from him and then berated herself for being so eager. Genny knew allowing herself to care would hurt even more when she did what she knew she must.

She waited as long as possible to call Sonya, fearful her plan would cause problems. Her suspicions Sonya had not forgotten were verified the moment she answered the phone.

"It certainly took you long enough to call. Is it a good time to visit?"

Genny twisted the telephone cord about her hand. "I'll be staying in Memphis for awhile longer."

"What about the meeting?" Sonya whined. "You promised."

"I told you I wouldn't abuse Stephen's kindness."

Another line rang, and Genny expected Sonya to say good-bye.

"Just hold on," she snapped.

Several minutes passed before she returned. "Look, Genny, you owe me this. I'll be there this weekend."

A shot of hurt spiraled through Genny. Not one word about her sister or nephew. They were only stepping-stones to the real prize. "I don't know if he'll be home."

"Then find out." The haughty demand carried a wealth of warning.

"I don't want to do this, Sonya. It reeks of deceit."

"Oh, please. It's business, plain and simple."

Somehow she would find a means of telling him what Sonya planned. "He checks in every day."

"Call the moment you hear," Sonya directed. "Tell him I'm coming for a visit."

Genny ended the conversation quickly. Allowing Sonya to coerce her had never been part of the plan. And she'd actually thought Sonya would forget if she delayed long enough. How could she be so naïve?

Stephen called later than usual to say they would be home Friday afternoon. "I thought we might run by the hospital and then go out to dinner."

"Sonya wants to come for a visit."

"The more the merrier. Want me to ask Ray along?"

"Are you sure?" *Idiot,* she chastised silently. *Tell Stephen the truth.*

"She's your sister." There was some hesitation before he admitted, "I'm not exactly endeared to her."

"There's a lot about Sonya you don't understand."

"How can you be so different?"

Maybe he'd understand if she explained Sonya might be less bitter if she had experienced love when she needed it most. But the past couldn't be rewritten and no matter how hard one fought to stop it from happening, it often affected the future.

"Stephen, you should know Sonya works for a PR firm in Nashville." There. It was out.

"That's nice."

"Did you hear what I said?"

"Sure. Sonya works for a PR firm."

"And that doesn't bother you?"

"Not particularly. I'm eager to get home."

He made it too easy. She hoped Stephen would realize what she was trying to tell him. "I can't wait for you to see Jonathan."

The conversation continued for a few more minutes before they said good night. Reluctantly, she dialed Sonya's condo, hoping to get the machine. *No such luck,* Genny thought glumly when Sonya answered on the third ring.

"It's about time you called. I turned down a dinner invitation and came straight home."

"Stephen just called. We're going to the hospital late Friday afternoon and then to dinner. He said to invite you along." A barrage of questions followed, most of which Genny couldn't answer.

"Do I need to give you a list?"

"I want no part in this."

"I'll meet you at the restaurant. I don't want to go to the hospital."

"But Sonya, you haven't seen Jonathan."

"You know how I hate hospitals."

"If that's what you want. See you Friday."

Sonya's attitude raised yet another important issue for Genny. What if something happened to her? Who would care for her baby?

On Friday, Genny spent the afternoon gardening. When the bus pulled up, Stephen jumped off and raced across the lawn, sweeping her into his arms and whirling her about.

Her love for the soil showed in the amount that clung to her old clothes. "You'll get dirty."

"I don't care."

He kissed her, and Genny's arms crept about his neck, and she kissed him back. The contact lasted for several heart-stopping seconds before catcalls from the bus forced her back to reality. She backed away.

"It's okay, Honey," Stephen said, taking her hand in his.

"Those clowns can't get out of the rain with directions."

He insisted Genny meet the guys and tugged her toward the bus. Her shyness was forgotten at their friendly reception.

They waved the bus off, and Stephen picked up his luggage.

Genny followed him to the house. "I'll change and meet you at the car. Sonya's going straight to the restaurant."

"Has she visited Jonathan yet?"

Genny shook her head. Afraid she would cry if they continued, she attempted escape.

"Wait. I have something for you."

She paused midflight, startled by the large box he placed in her arms. The beautifully wrapped package made a mockery of everything they had discussed.

Stephen tugged the artfully tied silk ribbon. Both watched it fall to the floor. A frown crept onto Genny's face when she recognized the logo on the box lid. He dropped the lid and folded back the tissue. Genny stared at the brilliant red suede.

"Take it out," he encouraged, doing it himself when she hesitated. He tossed the box onto the sofa and held the coat for her. "Slip your arm in." She did, surprised by how well it fit. "The color really suits you."

"You'll ruin it. I'm filthy."

"It'll clean."

She smoothed the sleeve of the fringed jacket and immediately fell in love. "It's beautiful but hardly practical. It must have cost the earth."

"You're worth every cent," Stephen said. "Wear it. For me."

"You can't buy me expensive presents."

"Actually I bought it for Jonathan. We can't have his mommy getting sick, can we?"

Their gazes locked.

"You know I have to wear it," Genny said, smiling sheepishly. "It's one of the most beautiful things I've ever seen."

Pleasure radiated across his face. "There's more." Tissue tumbled to the floor, and he held up a matching ankle-length skirt and blouse. "This is for taking such wonderful care of my home."

"For all you know, I robbed you blind and broke all your valuable art objects. Maybe I ran tours through here while you were away."

He laughed outright. "My riches extend to a tray of change on the dresser. I don't own any valuable art objects. The carpet's not worn or dirty, so I can rule out the tours. Just accept it as thanks for your help."

Thinking how she'd never had anything like this, Genny touched the soft material again. "Okay, but only because I don't want to embarrass you when we go out to dinner."

He looked surprised. "Why would you think that? Have I ever led you to believe I'm ashamed of you?"

"Well, no. . ."

"You could wear anything, and I'd never feel that way. Do you understand?" When she didn't respond, he continued, "I'm proud to be seen with you."

"You're a wonderful man. Too generous."

He chuckled at her words. "You had to get that in."

"I'll stop when you stop."

"Can't," Stephen said, shaking his head. "Get dressed, Woman. Meet me here at 4:30."

Genny raced home and into the shower. A few minutes later she combed tangles from her freshly washed hair. When it refused to be styled, Genny pulled it back with clasps. She reached for a bottle of foundation and smoothed the color on her face.

The suit fit as though made for her. Genny couldn't believe the difference in her appearance. Her self-confidence soared. Maybe clothes did make the woman.

She felt good enough to stand alongside her beautiful sister and not come up lacking. "God, forgive my vanity," Genny whispered, realizing the true reason had to do with her fears.

She wasn't suitable for Stephen, and yet she didn't want to give him up. Would he forget her existence when Sonya turned on the charm?

Stephen whistled when she stepped into the house. "You

really do something for that outfit."

Genny curtsied slightly. "Thank you, but it's the other way around."

"No, it's definitely you. You're beautiful. Those clothes couldn't look better on a high-dollar fashion model."

"Please, Stephen, plain old me isn't used to such surprises and compliments."

"But I thought you liked surprises," he said as they reached the car.

He looked confused and Genny sighed. She had been sending the wrong signals—saying no and then becoming as excited as a child over his gifts. "I like surprises, but yours take my breath away. I need to psych myself up. . .to prepare for your world."

Stephen glanced at her and said, "That's ridiculous."

A wave of anger surged through Genny. "I don't think so."

"Why do you persist in believing our worlds are so different?"

"Because they are. Meeting you is the stuff of fantasies."

"Genny, my life has been one huge surprise since you and Jonathan came into it. Nothing I do for you can compete. You've given one disillusioned man hope for his future."

Her mouth dropped open, and he tapped her chin. "Ready to visit Jonathan?"

At the hospital, reporters waylaid them. Lights flashed, and Genny flinched at the onslaught. Stephen pushed a camera to the side, sliding an arm about her waist and turning her toward him.

A reporter stalked them like a hungry predator. "Mr. Camden, we got a tip that there's a mystery woman in your life. Is this her?" she demanded, swinging the mike toward Genny.

"No comment. Keep walking," he instructed softly.

"Maybe if I explain," Genny said.

"It doesn't help. They draw their own conclusions."

"I'll make them understand." Genny turned to the reporter and said, "It's thanks to Mr. Camden that my son is alive today."

A man shoved his way to the front. "So why did he bring you into his home?"

Memories of another time when reporters had no intention of listening assailed Genny. She had wanted to explain then, but they preferred to focus on the horror of the act rather than the grief of two young women.

Stephen stepped forward. "Come on, people, you're making the lady nervous. I've never asked your permission before but if you feel the need to approve my staff. . ."

"Staff?"

"Yes, Mrs. Smith is my assistant."

"Smith?" a reporter cried, disbelief coloring his words. "Come on, what are you hiding?"

"Do your homework," Stephen countered, quelling the man with one look.

"Why do you need an assistant?"

"Why do you need one?"

Genny envied him the ease with which he fielded their questions.

"Praise God, Cowboy Jamboree is becoming more popular by the day. Mrs. Smith will help me respond to the mailbags filling my entry hall. As for why she's living in my guesthouse," he said, emphasizing the word, "she works a flexible shift so she can spend time with her son. Any more questions?"

"You plan to chase her around the desk?"

"Do I look like a woman men chase around desks?" Genny's droll question garnered a few chuckles. She glanced at Stephen, wondering if he'd picked up on their incredulity.

"Sorry, Ma'am. Looks like a wild-goose chase. Sorry to bother you, Mr. Camden. Perhaps we can get together for a personal interview?"

"Contact Chuck Harper."

Stephen hurried Genny into the hospital.

"Why did you lie to them? What will they think when Jonathan and I go home?"

"It's a serious offer, Genny. You need a job. I need an assistant.

I'm behind in my correspondence."

"You don't even know if I can type."

"Can you?"

"Well, yes, but. . ." He hadn't released his hold, and Genny felt winded by their rush down the hospital corridor. "You don't have to give me a job. I'll help you."

"Only if I pay you for your time."

"I'll think about it."

"Do that. Meanwhile, I'm going to chat with Mr. Harper. I warned him about the press."

"You can't be sure he did this."

Stephen's hold on her arm tightened. "You certainly can't be sure what he'll do or say next."

Inside the nursery, the media was forgotten when the nurse said Genny could hold Jonathan for the first time. Gowned, she held the infant as closely as possible, paying close attention to all the wires and tubes connected to him.

Stephen stood by her side, watching and smiling as she cooed words of love in a language only babies understood.

She glanced up. "Wish I had a camera. I'd love to show Sonya how he's grown."

Stephen glanced at the nurse. She nodded and returned a couple of minutes with an instant camera. "Hold him up."

Genny pulled Jonathan closer to her face and smiled. The woman laid the photo on the isolette before snapping another. "Mr. Camden, would you like to pose with them? I'm sure Mrs. Smith would like a picture for Jonathan's baby book."

"Can Stephen hold him?"

He shook his head and stepped back when the nurse said okay.

"It's not so hard," Genny prompted.

Stephen cradled the baby like a fine art object, concentration lines deepening along his brows and under his eyes. Genny adjusted his arm. "Don't worry. He won't break. Support his neck. You're doing great."

The time passed all too quickly. Tears came to her eyes

when they returned Jonathan to the isolette.

"Won't be long before he's home," Stephen assured, stripping off the gown. "Are you hungry?"

"I could eat."

Traffic was comparatively light, but they were still a few minutes late. Genny experienced a moment of dread when he parked. The feeling she didn't belong made her tense when Stephen reached for her hand.

"What's wrong?"

"This place must be popular," she managed.

"Mitch does okay. You're going to like this restaurant. The building has never been renovated. He says you don't make changes when something works. Ready?"

Sonya sat just inside the door, chatting with Ray. The two seemed to be very comfortable. Genny wished she felt that same comfort.

"What happened to you two?" Sonya demanded.

"Genny got to hold Jonathan for the first time," Stephen said. "The hostess will show you to our table. I need to speak to Ray."

Genny wondered what was so important as they followed the waiter across the room.

"Thanks for the opportunity to talk with Ray. I think maybe he's interested—" Sonya interrupted herself as she touched the fringed sleeve of Genny's coat. "Where did this come from?"

"A gift from Stephen." Genny slipped the jacket off and glanced around. "Does this place have a coat rack?"

"By the door, but I wouldn't suggest you leave it there. It would develop legs before dinner is served."

Genny draped the coat over the back of her chair. When Sonya asked to try it on, she placed a protective hand on the jacket. "Not tonight."

"Looks like you've hit pay dirt."

"Sonya!"

"I like nice things too. He knows what suits you."

Before she could comment, Stephen came up and rested his hands on Genny's shoulders.

"Stephen, this is my sister, Sonya Kelly. Sonya, this is Stephen Camden."

Sonya reached out her hand and flashed him her flirtatious smile. "My pleasure. Ray introduced himself when I gave the hostess my name."

After they were seated and studying the menus, Stephen glanced at Genny. "Order anything you want. Your doctor said you should gain some weight so indulge yourself."

"Not the beanpole," Sonya said with a disparaging laugh. "She's disgusting. Genny can eat anything and never gain a pound."

"I'm not so sure that's a positive," Stephen said. "A few extra pounds would have made things easier for her with Jonathan."

Genny noted the way Sonya's eyebrows lifted at his protective words.

"Oh, that reminds me." Genny pulled her purse around and retrieved the snapshots. "I want to show you how Jonathan's grown."

Sonya didn't bother to take them. Genny noted Ray's sympathetic look when he reached out. "Steve brags about how big he's getting." One by one, he flipped through the photos. "Mighty handsome boy, Genny. Here, Ms. Kelly, take a look at your nephew."

"Oh, call me Sonya, please." The pictures fell to the table-top with barely a glance before she said, "Looks like he'll be in the hospital for awhile."

An uncomfortable silence followed the insensitive comment.

"He's improving every day," Genny whispered.

Stephen's hand covered hers on the tabletop. Once the orders were taken, Ray asked Sonya to dance.

"Not the nurturing sort, is she?" Stephen asked as the couple moved out of hearing range.

Genny picked up the pictures, a frown creasing her forehead.

'I don't understand her aversion. He's not repulsive or anything. Why is she like that?"

"Honey, don't let Sonya upset you."

"I don't know what I expect from her. She never refers to
him as anything but 'the baby' or my son. He's her nephew.
Why doesn't she care? I would if he were her child."

"Could be she doesn't want to share center stage with
Jonathan."

Genny twisted in her seat and glanced at the dance floor.
Sonya flirted with Ray, oblivious to the hurt she had caused.

"Probably," she agreed with a slight shrug of her shoulders.
"We need to discuss what you told the reporters."

The waiter's quick reappearance with their food was
another perk of celebrity status.

"Not now we don't." Stephen said grace and took a bite of
chicken. "Just like my grandma used to make."

Genny's brows shot up with her surprise. Of course, he had
parents and grandparents. "Is she a great cook?"

"The best. Mom's idea of Southern-fried chicken is take-
out," he said with an indulgent smile.

"Do your parents live in Memphis?" As soon as the words
left her mouth, Genny wished she could draw them back.
Questions begat questions. She wasn't ready to tell him the
story of her life.

"They're in Houston. I can't wait to introduce you and
Jonathan to them. What about yours?"

"Dead."

"I'm sorry."

"Sorry about what?" Sonya asked as Ray pulled out her chair.

"Genny told me about your parents."

"Did you. . ." Sonya stopped when Genny flashed her a
warning glare. "Oh, never mind. It's old news."

"Excuse me, please," Genny said. "I need the ladies' room."

She returned to find Sonya wearing her coat.

"I was cold," Sonya said. "Stephen said it was okay."

Genny felt betrayed.

"What I said was it would be okay if you thought Genny wouldn't mind."

She experienced mixed emotions. Genny didn't want Sonya wearing her coat, but she didn't want to be selfish either. "It's okay. She's cold. Please be careful with it, Sonya."

No doubt she would hear from Sonya later, but the coat was hers. And she didn't want to share.

After a few initial false starts at conversation, dinner was consumed in silence. Not an impressive first meeting.

"I don't know about the rest of you, but I'm all for calling it a night," Stephen announced.

"But it's early," Sonya protested, sounding disappointed.

Sonya's nervous behavior didn't bode well. "Could we all go back to your place and visit? I wanted to spend time with Genny. Maybe see where she's living."

Genny almost screamed. Why couldn't Sonya leave well enough alone? Stephen wasn't stupid. He'd see right through her pitiful little act.

"Sure. You can follow us to the house."

Ray opted to head for home and wished them all good night. At the house, Sonya followed Stephen to the door with Genny bringing up the rear.

"I live in the guesthouse, Sonya. Let's go over there."

"Oh, but I want to see Steve's home." She wrapped her hand about his arm and smiled up at him. "You don't mind, do you?"

He didn't look too pleased. "Come in. I'll fix some coffee."

Sonya's gaze roamed about the beautifully decorated room. She waited until he left then said, "You've certainly done well for us."

"There's no us involved in this," Genny muttered, lowering her voice as she glanced toward the kitchen. "And cut the theatrics. You're being way too obvious."

"You'd better remember who's taking care of you and your brat," Sonya hissed. "I don't work all the time for pleasure."

Furious, Genny growled, "I thought you did. We're not destitute. We have John's Social Security, and I plan to work."

"Well, aren't we full of ourselves today?" Sonya's sarcasm strengthened as she continued. "You'd better watch that smart mouth. And I don't appreciate you making a fool out of me over that coat. You better hope it didn't hurt my plan."

Tears stung Genny's eyes. She was so tired of being afraid.

"I got a lead on a killer investment that's going to take all my savings. My budget won't stretch to cover your needs." Sonya drew a quick breath and continued. "I've considered what you can do and have a possible lead. One of the guys at work knows someone who needs a housekeeper. He thinks the couple would let you take the baby along—as long as he doesn't interrupt your work." Sonya shrugged as she worried over one of her perfectly manicured nails. "They're away all day anyway so they wouldn't know if you didn't tell them. And the good news is they want someone to start immediately." A little laugh escaped her. "They're so desperate for good help, they're planning to add on quarters for a housekeeper."

Tears flowed freely, as Genny fought back the sobs that rose in her throat. How could Sonya be so lacking in compassion? John repeatedly did favors for her sister. How could she repay them like this?

"She won't be needing your money," Stephen announced, slamming the coffee tray onto the side table and pulling Genny's trembling body into his arms. "It's okay, Baby."

"You misunderstood."

"I understand perfectly. I've never met anyone so heartless."

"I'm trying to help," Sonya said.

Anger sparked in the gray eyes. "You haven't taken care of Genny."

"I resent that."

"He doesn't mean it," Genny soothed, flashing him a warning frown.

"She should have been there for you."

"Genny knows I have to work to keep a roof over our heads. She's welcome to leave any time she feels she can do better."

They glared at each other, foes in a battle Genny felt powerless to stop. "She won't trouble you any longer. I'll take care of her and Jonathan."

"So Genny's going to become a kept woman," Sonya jibed. "Why doesn't that surprise me?"

Genny caught Stephen's arm when he took a step forward. "Genny has a job—with room and board. Your friends can build their housekeeper quarters for someone else."

"Why didn't you tell me?" Sonya demanded.

"Because it's none of your business," Stephen countered. "We haven't discussed the specifics yet. And you owe Genny an apology. That 'kept woman' comment was totally out of line."

"It doesn't matter," Genny said, silently pleading with Stephen to stop his tirade.

"She has no right to talk to you that way."

Sonya's expression spoke her opinion of his viewpoint.

Despair filled Genny. "Just stop!" she screamed. "I can't stand any more." She charged from the room.

What was he thinking? Genny felt a little crazed. Her life whirled like an out of control merry-go-round. Where would it all stop?

⟡

"Well, isn't she a bundle of surprises?" Sonya exclaimed. "I never thought she had it in her."

"If you ever speak to her like that again, I'll make sure you regret it," Stephen said, abandoning all pretense.

"Don't threaten me. I know my sister. What happens when you tire of her? Don't expect me to pick up the pieces. Again."

"Like you have this time?" Stephen asked, his tone laced with heavy sarcasm. "No, Sonya, I don't think you know Genny at all."

ten

Heart pounding, Stephen burst into the guesthouse without knocking. He skidded to a halt before Genny. "I'm sorry."

She glared at him. "Just what are you trying to prove?"

"That you don't have to be dependent on that woman ever again. I'm offering independence, a job, and a place for you and your son to live without fear, without threats."

"What, Stephen? What can I possibly do to repay you? Do you have any idea what you're taking on?"

He hesitated. Should he just stay out of it? Leave her to make her own way? No. Jonathan wouldn't end up like Bobby.

The poignant story of his former band member's life tore at his heart. He hadn't listened to Bobby's cries for help. None of the guys wanted to baby-sit the barely twenty-one-year-old kid when he joined the band. They were too easygoing about his wild lifestyle, alcohol, and suspected drugs, only telling him to lay off when they should have insisted he get help.

Stephen's guilt had increased the night he packed Bobby's meager possessions and found the tattered sheet of paper in his friend's wallet. A letter from his mother dated a few days after his birth explaining why she had given him up.

Lack of money had been no excuse as far as Stephen was concerned. He blamed Bobby's mother, certain she could have found a way. But after meeting Genny, and witnessing her method of survival, he felt differently. Telling himself the two situations had nothing to do with each other didn't work. He wanted to help because he cared for Genny and her son. But he needed to do this—for Bobby.

"Let's just say I'm doing it for a friend. I've met a woman I like and respect." Her expression softened when he admitted, "I'm attracted to you. And I think you're attracted to me.

But I'm on the road and you're here, struggling to support Jonathan, and I'm afraid circumstances will prevail. I can't help but worry. What would happen if you couldn't provide for Jonathan? If you had to put him in foster care?"

Genny's horrified expression told him losing Jonathan was something she hadn't considered. Stephen sat down and drew her into a hug. "You won't take money from me. Why not a job?"

"You've done so much. I don't want you to—"

"You think this is some trumped-up way of giving you money?" he interrupted. When she nodded, he insisted, "It's a real job. The fan mail is backing up while I'm on the road. If you don't believe me, come over to the house. I'll show you."

"I'm not a fast typist," Genny protested.

Her resolve is weakening. "We'll work out a plan."

"There's Jonathan. Once he's released, I can't take him to an office every day. Day care isn't a good choice either."

"You're putting up stumbling blocks. You can work here or at the house."

She stood and walked over to the fireplace. With her back to him, she said, "Oh, Stephen, I don't know."

"This isn't spur-of-the-moment, Genny. It's been on my mind during this last tour. I need someone and so do you. To put it simply, I like coming home to you and Jonathan."

Intense astonishment touched her pale face as she whirled to face him. "I don't think it's such a good idea for you to become more attached to us."

"We're single adults, Genny."

"I'm an older adult with a child."

"It's not an insurmountable number of years, and I love Jonathan. So where's the problem?"

⁂

Genny felt stunned by Stephen's admitted attraction. "Just how involved are you planning on becoming in Jonathan's life?"

"As involved as you'll allow."

Genny lifted a photo from the mantel and studied her son.

"He may be a baby, but he's very aware of people around him. I'm worried he'll become too attached to you."

"Would that be so bad?"

It could be. Genny considered how much losing him would affect them both. "Maybe the years aren't such a big deal now," she argued. "But one day you'll want a child of your own. I see how you look at Jonathan. I know how important children are to a man. His children, not another man's."

Walking to where she stood, Stephen said, "For the first time in my life I'm thinking I'd like to be a father. But I'm not asking for anything more than a chance to spend time with you. Jonathan could use a man's influence in his life."

Back when she'd first married, Genny dreamed of the perfect family—happily married parents and two children. Reality took a radical turn with John's death.

"You'd be a wonderful father. So wonderful I can't let you get mixed up with my crazy life. There's a woman out there who can give you the special world you deserve." Her hand slipped to his cheek. "You won't find her if you don't look, and you can't look if you're with us."

"Let the future take care of itself." Stephen had used the same words only days before when he'd done his part to shape their future.

She felt so confused. She wanted his caring, but she needed her independence. Genny doubted she could have both. Stephen made her feel too safe and secure. "You don't understand," she protested.

"I do, Genny. Just don't feel guilty if the happiness you deserve comes quicker than expected."

"I'm not ready for a relationship, and I don't think you should wait until I am."

"I understand fear." Stephen retreated to the sofa and stared down at the hands that dangled between his parted thighs. The prolonged silence raised all kinds of doubts for Genny. He looked up, the gray eyes blazing with his inner fire. "More than you realize. Don't think I haven't been tempted to run the other way. But I can't. You draw me back. I can't leave again without knowing you're safe and secure. Hearing your sister tell you there's no money in her budget for your needs makes it even more urgent. I feel responsible for you already."

His words provoked her ire. "No one's responsible for me but me. Understand that, Stephen. No one. I won't be taken care of. I'm not the child."

"And I'm not the enemy. Take the job, Genny. We have all the time you need."

Her mind spun with her bewilderment. It would be too easy to accept. For Jonathan's sake. For her own. But what about Stephen? "It's not fair to you."

"Let me worry about myself. I know what makes me happy, and right now, I want to see you smile."

"And what about next week? The month after that?"

"I'm not into living for tomorrow, Genny. God tells me to take it one day at a time."

She stared at him, not really startled by his revelation. Admittedly, there was something between them—feelings stronger than friendship and her overwhelming guilt. Genny had never felt so torn. She had to keep John Smith's memory alive for his son. She owed him that much. Could she do that if she allowed her feelings for Stephen to grow? Did she have to face a future void of masculine attention in order to do that?

"What's going on here?"

Their attention turned to Sonya.

Sonya's gaze moved from one to the other. "You'd better think about this. You can't afford to be impulsive." She turned toward the door and then back. "You really need to get right on that housekeeper position. My friend doesn't think it will stay open very long."

Rebellion bubbled and overflowed as Genny understood the warning in Sonya's words. She refused to be manipulated any longer. She turned to Stephen, to the warmth in his gray gaze. If his eyes contained just a glimpse of the world he offered, they hinted at paradise.

His brow lifted, and he reached out to her. "Genny's going to accept my offer, aren't you, Genny?"

She took his hand. "Yes, Stephen."

Sonya shrugged. "I've got a long drive."

"Good-bye, Sonya."

The door slammed shut behind her. Stephen's arm slipped about Genny's shoulder. A deep sigh slid from her, and she wilted beneath his touch.

"Are you okay?"

Genny looked him in the eye. "I haven't been totally honest with you. Sonya has high aspirations—sees herself as an executive. She insisted that I help her."

"Help her how?"

"She wants to convince you to change PR firms. She's been on my case ever since she realized who you were, reminding me babies aren't cheap and saying if I expected her to help, we'd need a larger income. I'm sorry."

Stephen shrugged the words away. "Sonya plays on your insecurities. You don't need her anymore."

It sounded too wonderful to be true. She needed a break from Sonya. Some days she didn't think she could bear another threat or cruel comment. But what if Sonya's predictions came true? What would happen when Stephen wanted her and Jonathan out of his life?

"There's nothing I want as much as to regain control of my life, but I'm not sure I can swing it. Once I leave here, I have to consider how far the money will stretch."

Stephen pushed her chin up. "Genny, listen to me. I'm not turning you out in six weeks or six months. The place is yours for as long as you need it."

"You have a life, Stephen. How will you explain us to your friends?" Particularly the female ones. Genny didn't care for the surge of jealousy that spiraled through her at the thought of Stephen with other women.

"Why don't we cross that bridge when we get there? Mrs. James will appreciate your help taking care of the place.

Actually it's her house," he joked. "She spends more time here than me." The anguish in his voice made Genny ache. "There's a housekeeping fund. I'll authorize you to make withdrawals for groceries and miscellaneous expenses."

"I can pay for groceries and electricity. It's only fair."

"I prefer to cover room and board while you're house-sitting. After that, we'll work out an arrangement."

"Stephen, about the letters. . . I've never done any real office work."

"Just read the letters, answer those you can, and put aside the ones you feel you can't handle. As long as you don't book us anywhere or tell people where I live, I foresee no problems. If you want, I'll ask the other guys if they want you to handle their fan mail."

"I thought I would be answering mail for the whole band."

Stephen shook his head. "I can't speak for the whole group. Well, Gen, what do you think?"

What did she think? On one hand, it was as if she'd stumbled onto a pot of gold. She kept expecting to blink her eyes and find it had disappeared. On the other hand, she was afraid it would turn out to be fool's gold. Still, she recognized the job was ideal for her.

Stephen offered the opportunity to earn a salary and maybe even to relieve his burden in some small way. "When do I start?"

The corners of his eyes crinkled with his pleased smile. "Officially, you already have."

"What about the letters? I could start on those now if you show me what to do."

"You need to take it easy for awhile longer," he warned. "There's a lot of mail to sort through. We'll see how it goes before I ask the other guys. Of course, there would be a salary adjustment if you take on anyone else's mail."

"You're being more than generous."

Stephen took her hands in his. "You'd be doing more work."

She grew serious. "Please understand that I'm not unappreciative. I feel I'm taking advantage of your good nature."

Stephen shook his head. "I'm not doing anything I don't want to do. Remember that, Genny. Having you here has been good for me. You've motivated me to think about what God wants me to do with my life. . .from considering my career choices to dedicated prayer time. Whatever He intends, there's no question He'll provide as well. I'd better get out of here so you can get to bed. Don't worry. Okay?"

"You make it hard to do that. Particularly when you pulverize my every care with your solutions."

"I'm sorry about Sonya. Maybe she'll be more human now that her burden has been lightened."

Burden. No matter whose lips it came from, the word was as deadly as an untreated rattlesnake bite. Genny's eyelids dropped to hide her hurt.

Genevieve Smith had a goal too. One day she would be self-sufficient. No one's burden. No one's responsibility. And she intended to see that it came sooner than later.

eleven

After Stephen left, Genny found herself considering Sonya's little jab about making a career of being a housewife. It wasn't the first time she'd heard the words.

John's firm had been retained by her parents to renovate their house. With Sonya away at college, Genny had no competition for his attentions, and he quickly became a good friend, a confidant when times were difficult, and eventually the man she loved with all her heart. John knew where he was going, and at seventeen, she already she knew she wanted to go with him.

The job was partially completed when Sonya came home for Thanksgiving and her interest in the handsome contractor became obvious. When Genny told her she loved John, Sonya insisted he was too old for her. Genny met Sonya's threats to tell their parents with the firm resolve that they wouldn't change her mind. Sonya became even more determined, flaunting her beauty and flirting outrageously. Genny didn't doubt John felt flattered by Sonya's attention and prepared to fight for her love. But then Sonya returned to college.

When she chose to marry John, Sonya accused her of looking for a father figure. The ten-year age difference meant nothing to Genny. Still, John insisted they wait until she turned eighteen before he proposed officially.

The thought of how her parents rushed things along made Genny shudder. John had been supportive, moving her in with him and seeing to it that she took her finals and received her diploma. He insisted she have her own room until they were married. She found happiness in the haven of his home.

For more than seventeen years, she put everything into being John Smith's wife. From the moment she accepted his proposal, housewife and mother had been her choice. John's ability to support them comfortably made the decision easy.

Genny knew she wanted it more because she'd never experienced a true family life. Her children would never know the loneliness of parents more involved with their careers than their children. John agreed it was important that their children have their mother home. Her efforts to make their home a happy place worked for years, until the perfection cracked about the edges when the family refused to arrive.

When John's behavior changed, she hoped it had more to do with the pressures of work than marital problems. He stayed on edge, and at times she felt every word he exchanged with her was snapped or growled. The least little thing pushed them toward arguments of major proportions.

Arguments she refused to participate in, always walking away until he was willing to talk reasonably. Secretly, she blamed herself for the changes.

And then her pregnancy changed everything. John's response was incredible. He became more loving and caring, responsive to her needs, and was home every night. When her doctor expressed concern about her age and health, she agreed to the battery of tests at John's urging. He insisted she focus on delivering a healthy child, and Genny reveled in his loving.

Her life took another unexpected turn with his death and the return of loneliness. Until she met Stephen. He forced her to confront her feelings. Genny cared deeply for him. If she admitted the truth, she loved him, but the feeling it was too soon tormented her.

But what could she do? Despair grasped Genny in its clutches, reminding her of times barely past. She fell to her knees and prayed aloud, "Father in heaven, thank You for all the miraculous gifts You bestow upon me daily. Thank You for the beautiful son You have given me. Please help him to grow and strengthen in Your love.

"Your lost child comes to You tonight seeking guidance. Confusion and hurt separated me from You. I don't want to ask why, but because I'm human I find myself doing exactly that. Now You've sent another wonderful man into my life, and I find myself at a loss as to how to deal with the situation. If You mean for Stephen to be part of our lives, help me accept and understand Your will. Amen."

Afterward, she stood and walked toward the bathroom. For the first time in weeks, she felt a sense of relief.

❧

Stephen returned to the house and went straight to the telephone. "I warned you about the reporters."

"What reporters?" Chuck Harper asked.

"The ones you sent."

"It wasn't me."

Stephen frowned. If it wasn't Chuck Harper, then how had they learned about Genny? How had they known to go to the hospital? A seed of suspicion planted itself. Only a few people knew their whereabouts, and Genny admitted to coercion by Sonya. Had they planned the incident? No, not Genny. She had told him about Sonya's plans.

"They'll be contacting you about an interview," Stephen said. "Find out who their source was."

"Sure. You plan to do the interview?" Chuck asked curiously.

"On my terms. With no reference to a mystery woman in my life," Stephen emphasized.

"What role is she playing?"

The man's question raised Stephen's resentment. He wished he understood why Chuck Harper set his teeth on edge. "It's not your concern."

"A lot of female fans like the fact that you're a single man," the manager reminded. "That makes it my concern."

Stephen sighed and muttered, "Genny's taking over my fan mail."

"Is that all she's taken over?"

The man never let anything drop. "She's a special woman," he admitted. "I care a lot for her and her son. I won't see either of them hurt."

After hanging up, Stephen went into the bedroom. He

pulled a photo of Genny and Jonathan from his coat pocket and stared at the smiling twosome.

What a beautiful baby Jonathan was. Stephen felt a sudden longing to hold a child of his own, something he'd never experienced before. Wives and kids were demanding, and he led a bachelor's life, following his career with unequaled desire for anything else.

He'd never felt any similar desire when holding his sister's babies. Why now?

❧

Stephen left for the next tour dates and honoring his insistence that she rest, Genny often reclined in bed or rested on the sofa as she separated the contents of the mailbags.

Aware she should be happy, Genny found she fretted about everything. She wanted her baby home. She wanted her relationship with Sonya worked out. And she wanted to get some sort of perspective she could live with on her feelings for Stephen.

As she prepared for her checkup, Genny could almost recite what the doctor was going to say. She'd lost five sorely needed pounds, her face was gaunt, her cheekbones even more prominent. And what her doctor didn't say, Stephen was sure to add the moment he laid eyes on her.

She bundled into her coat and braved the dropping temperatures to race to the car. After allowing the engine to warm up, Genny turned the heat to high, rubbing her hands together to get the circulation going. She'd opted to go to her regular gynecologist instead of the doctor who delivered Jonathan.

During the long drive, she debated going by Sonya's office after her visit. Would the visit cause another scene? For that matter, would Sonya even talk to her? She abhorred the idea of never speaking with her sister again. Family was important. She wanted Jonathan to know his aunt.

Dr. Rainer was enthusiastic about Jonathan's progress. "At this rate, he'll be a butterball before long. Now let's see how you're doing, young lady."

The 'young lady' brought a smile to her face. Genny wondered how old she would be before he stopped calling her that.

After the exam, Genny waited in his office, considering how much her life had changed since she last sat in the same chair. That day she'd asked about the trip that turned her life around. Her thoughts drifted to Stephen.

She wondered where he was, smiling as she considered she only had to check the schedule. Within hours they would chat on the phone. What would he say tonight?

Dr. Rainer closed the door. She jumped, a guilty smile curving her lips. "Why so fidgety, Genevieve?" He settled in the chair, his gaze on her chart. "You've lost too much weight, and you're anemic."

She squirmed, glad the man couldn't tell what was on her mind. "Everything's fine. In fact, I started work. I'm answering fan mail for Stephen Camden."

The doctor cocked an eyebrow. "The singer?"

"He's been wonderful," Genny enthused, tucking her hair behind her ear. "Stephen was there when Jonathan was born."

He nodded his satisfaction. "Glad you've met someone."

"We're only friends," Genny offered.

"Too bad. A good man would do you a world of good. You're perfectly healthy except for the anemia and needing to gain a few pounds. We can remedy that with good food and vitamins. And from the look on your face when you talk about this singer fellow, I'd say he could make you happy."

"It's not that sort of relationship," she objected.

"You're a young woman. You'll marry again. Probably give Jonathan a brother or sister."

His words hit her. "Is that really a possibility? I mean. . . Well, it took so long to conceive. . . And with Jonathan being premature, I thought. . ."

Dr. Rainer had no time for her stumbling words. "I don't see any problem."

Genny accepted the vitamin samples. Dr. Rainer had been

her doctor forever. He'd done her physicals, counseled them on infertility, and cared for her during pregnancy. Now he seemed to think it logical she would have a relationship with another man. But not just any ordinary man—handsome, successful Stephen Camden.

In the car, her thoughts went to what he'd said. *Is he right about the possibility of my having another child? Could I still have the babies I've dreamed of?* A vision of Stephen with Jonathan popped into her head. He would make a great father. *With the right woman,* she warned herself.

But why couldn't that woman be me? Why do I persist in believing we can't have a future? Because Stephen is excitement personified while I am as tame as a toothless tiger, she thought with a wry smile.

Besides, the thought was ridiculous. The odds of finding herself the winner of a million-dollar sweepstakes were higher. All women had fantasies, and just because Stephen was helping hers along didn't mean he could ever love her.

She drove to Sonya's office. As much as Genny dreaded the confrontation, she knew she had to at least try.

Sonya was probably right. Stephen's interest would wane, and she'd be right back where she started. Genny brushed away a tear. She hated the uncertainty that tore at her. Why couldn't she accept God's promise that she need not worry about tomorrow?

Another secretary occupied the front desk and directed Genny to the conference room where Sonya assembled press packets. "Hello, Sonya."

"I wondered when you'd show up. Mr. High-and-mighty give you your walking papers?"

The fury in Sonya's tone surprised her. "I thought it would be a good idea if we talked. Things didn't go well the other night at Stephen's."

"Don't mention his name to me," Sonya snapped.

"Why can't you be happy for me?" Genny asked. "Aren't you the least bit thankful to him for all he's done to help me?"

Sonya slammed the handfuls of paper down on the conference table and shoved her long blond hair over her shoulder. "Genny, you don't even know the man."

"I know enough."

"He doesn't know you either. I bet you've never told him your disgusting little secret. Did you ever tell him exactly how our parents died?"

Genny forced herself to remain calm. "What's really bothering you, Sonya? Are you concerned that I could get hurt? Or that you didn't help me?"

"I gave you a lead on a job."

"The only job you considered me qualified for?"

Sonya glowered at her. "It's not like you have any other skills."

She registered the sarcasm. Sonya considered her ungrateful. "You know I can't leave Jonathan. Why are you so determined something bad is going to come from Stephen helping me?"

"Because I'm a lot wiser about the world." Sonya walked across the room and lifted a folder from the credenza. She flung it onto the table. "See for yourself."

Clippings flowed over the slick surface of the mahogany conference table. Genny caught one just before it floated off the table and laid the paper down without looking at it. "Why?"

"To prove he's no different from the others." Sonya quickly spread them about. "Look at the number of women. It's not all fun and games. People get hurt. It could be you."

Sonya considered her naïve. Maybe Genny didn't know a lot about Stephen, but she did know his intentions were honorable. Sonya's condemnation of every plan she made for her future played a huge role in her confusion. She didn't feel Sonya was being cautious. Nor did she want to accept that Sonya preferred her weak and at her mercy.

Genny pulled from the reserve of strength deep within her. She wasn't an idiot. The grief and problems since John's death made her look like one, and maybe it was taking her too long to get back to her feet, but she would stand tall again.

"I know everything I need to know about Stephen."

"You'd choose him over family?" Sonya asked, her fisted hands pressing into the back of a padded chair.

"If you force me to. I owe Stephen a lot, Sonya. He didn't have to do all he's done."

"And I did?"

Genny didn't flinch as she met Sonya's gaze straight on. "If the situations were reversed and your child was lying in the hospital, you wouldn't need to depend on the kindness of strangers. I'd be there for you."

Sonya bristled and roughly stuffed the papers back into the folder. "I've been there for you."

Genny shook her head. "You've shown your true feelings every step of the way. I took Stephen's job to take the burden off you. I don't want you to feel forced to take care of us when you obviously resent it so much. For some reason you pretend Jonathan is nonexistent. You never ask about him. You've never seen him. I'm not sure why, but it's your loss. My son is a beautiful child. You should know I confessed the truth to Stephen about your visit and my involvement."

"I told him, and I'll tell you," Sonya yelled. "After it's over, you'll come running back to me. You're too weak to stand on your own. Just remember my house is not a hotel. You and your baby won't be welcome there in the future."

Her words had the same effect as water on dying embers, outing the feeble flame that struggled to survive.

"I won't impose on you again." Like a diver cutting his air hose underwater, dread surged through her. *Please God, let it be so.*

"It's your funeral."

A picture of Stephen wrapped in a woman's arms taunted her from the tabletop. Genny didn't have to read the articles to learn of the band's wild antics. But instinct told her Stephen was a good man.

"Since you won't be returning, I'd appreciate you getting the rest of your stuff out of my house."

Sonya's caustic tone ate a hole in Genny's heart. "I'll take care of it this week and leave the key on the kitchen counter."

"It'll be wonderful not to feel so cramped."

"Forgive my intrusion on your wonderful life," Genny managed, masking her hurt with the same sarcasm Sonya showed.

"Oh, cut the theatrics, Genny. You can pretend everything is perfect but the truth of the matter is that your life is going to be a lot harder than you've ever imagined. How you think you'll work and tend to that sick kid is beyond me."

"The Lord will make a way." Genny realized she actually believed that.

"Yeah, like the Lord has ever done a lot for either of us," Sonya said. Laughter accompanied the disrespectful words. "I've got work to do."

Genny couldn't get out of the building fast enough. She raced to the car and climbed inside, breathing deeply as she fought back the tears. When would she ever learn? There was only one person in the entire world Sonya cared about—herself. Her sister shared that trait with their parents. They hadn't cared that they were destroying their children, and Sonya didn't care that she broke Genny's heart.

❧

That night, Stephen accepted the outcome of the meeting with an offer to help her move.

"I'd better get to work. My doctor's appointment put me behind."

"What did he say?" Stephen asked.

His not-so-casual question reminded her of the doctor's words. "I need to gain weight. He gave me vitamins and a prescription for iron tablets. Otherwise, I'm perfectly healthy."

She didn't tell him about the doctor's recommendation that she get on with her life, his suggestion that a good man would do her a world of good.

"Okay, I'll work on a truck."

"Thanks, Stephen," she whispered, once more reassured that she'd made the right choice.

"See you soon."

twelve

Stephen gestured to the two men standing behind him. "The guys volunteered to help."

Ray glanced at Kyle. "That's what he's calling it now."

"Hey, I only asked to borrow your truck," Stephen defended.

"And I go where my truck goes," Ray said. "Where do we start?"

"Why don't you and Kyle take the crib apart while I give Genny a hand with the other stuff?"

The two men shared a knowing look. "Good thing you bought your tools along," Ray told Kyle.

"I had an idea he'd pull something like this."

"Yeah, he can tear up a guitar, but he's dangerous with tools."

"Come on, guys, you're making me look bad here."

Genny moved to Stephen's side. "You didn't force them to help, did you?"

The men laughed.

"You can't make these guys do anything. They're the ones who insisted it wouldn't take as long with three sets of hands. By the way, this is Kyle. He's part of our road crew."

Genny shook his hand. "We've met before. I made you nervous."

Kyle grinned. "Good thing Steve was there. I was pretty useless."

"You pitched right in, just like today. Thank you both. Let me show you the crib."

Stephen caught her hand. "They can find it. Top of the stairs to the right. Big wooden thing with bars."

"You're such a comedian," Ray said, leading the way.

Stephen followed Genny into the kitchen. A box filled with baby items sat on the counter.

"Only a couple more things and I'll be done here," Genny said, reaching into the cabinet.

They worked quickly, and Genny wasn't surprised to find her meager collection of possessions barely filled half of Ray's truck bed. Paying their debts had been an honor thing for her. Almost every possession she owned, including the rings on her fingers, had been sold. The few salvaged pieces had more sentimental than financial value.

While checking to assure everything was packed, Stephen spotted some boxes in the back of the closet. "What about these?"

The cardboard containers held the things Genny had used to make her place a home. "My favorite cookbooks. Gardening books. Christmas ornaments. A couple of porcelain pieces my grandparents gave me. An afghan I knitted. I need to check on storage space."

"Why?" Stephen dragged them from the closet. "They'll give the guesthouse your personal touch. Make it more like home for you and Jonathan."

"I won't be there that long."

He glanced over his shoulder. "These things obviously mean something to you. Why not enjoy them?"

"You don't mind?"

Stephen hefted the closest one. "I want you to think of my home as yours. Understand?"

Genny nodded, and he left to carry the boxes downstairs. She vacuumed the carpet and checked one last time to make certain everything was the same as when Sonya said there was no other option but for Genny to live with her. Had it really been such a short time? It seemed more like a lifetime.

She no longer had to tolerate Sonya's abuse, and though she had no idea what the future held for her and Jonathan, Genny felt thrilled by the prospect of moving on with her life. The most frightening aspect was the developing relationship between her and Stephen.

He'd broken through her reserve and made her care about

him. Though Stephen insisted the future would take care of itself, Genny's self-doubts made her question why he helped. Only time would provide the answer, but she realized something else. She loved having someone who cared, and if it were only days or weeks, she wasn't going to refuse his friendship.

"Genny, let's go," Stephen called. "Everything's loaded."

She hurried down the stairs, encountering air as she neared the bottom.

"Well, hello," Stephen exclaimed, surprise in his gray gaze when she landed against his chest. His arms secured her against his body, her feet dangling uselessly as Genny grabbed his shoulders to keep from falling.

"I missed the last stair."

Stephen's lips brushed hers and lingered before he pulled back and flashed her a teasing grin. "And here I thought you were really glad to see me."

Always. She almost spoke the word out loud. "I'm surprised I didn't knock the breath out of you."

He laughed and set her on the floor. "We need to concentrate on fattening you up. Either that or buy you lead-soled shoes to keep you from floating off."

"Good luck," Genny said as she pulled on her jacket. "My mother used to complain I was hopeless."

"You've never been any larger than now?"

"Well, if you recall a short time ago I resembled a baby whale, but you could say I've reverted to normal."

He smiled and dropped one eyelid in a way that made Genny's heart palpitate. "We'll soon have you so happy you'll have to work out at the gym."

"You can try." Genny worked the key around the ring and slipped it off. "I told Sonya I'd leave this on the counter." *Why don't I just tell him I can't go through with it?* Genny asked for the millionth time. Surely he could understand her doubts. Their kisses could be a prelude to something bigger than the both of them.

"You're not sure about this, are you?"

"Not completely," she answered truthfully. "I want to be close to Jonathan and earn my own way, but. . ."

"You don't want to interfere with my life," Stephen guessed.

"Yes. . . I mean, no. . . We don't want to stand in the way of your happiness."

"Think of this as your first steps toward independence."

"I can do that. If you allow me to work toward that goal."

Stephen kissed her forehead and rested an arm about her shoulders. "Okay, let's hit the road."

The guys had unloaded most of the stuff when they arrived at the house. "We can finish this if you want to go over to the hospital," Stephen said as he parked.

"If you don't mind. Just stack everything. I'll put it away when I get home."

He left the keys in the ignition. "Have fun. Oh, give this to Jonathan with my love." Stephen kissed her, and Genny sat there for a moment longer wondering how she would explain such a kiss to her infant son.

❧

Two hours later, Genny returned home to find Stephen had done more than place her possessions in the guesthouse. The boxes sat in the various rooms, waiting to be put away.

He was in the process of taking a box of personal items into the bathroom. "I'll start the tub for you. I'm going to tackle the crib."

"You'll need help holding the pieces."

"Go," he said, pushing her toward the bathroom. "I can manage."

Relaxing in the warm water melted away the stresses of the day. Genny soaked, loath to move, even to soap herself. She could hear Stephen next door, and her lips twitched as he grumbled his way through the task he assigned himself.

He tapped on the door. "You've been in there long enough."

"Spoilsport," Genny murmured, using the hand spray to rinse bubbles from her body.

"I heard that. Get dressed and come over to the house for dinner."

❧

Stephen glanced up when Genny entered the kitchen. Her skin was rosy-hued, strands of damp hair clung to her neck where it had slipped from the rubber band she'd worn all day, and she'd thrown on a pair of jeans and a shirt. She looked beautiful to him. Struck by the depth of his feelings for her, he sucked in a deep breath. "I finished the crib, but you should check it for sturdiness before you put Jonathan in."

"I'm sure you did fine," Genny said, joining him at the island. "What can I do to help?"

❧

Life settled into a routine. Genny kept the home fires burning while Stephen went out on tour again. He was due home that afternoon, which was a good thing. A surprise delivery of baby furniture and clothes—good quality, expensive things she could never afford on her salary—required an immediate discussion.

The dashboard clock caught her eye, and Genny panicked. Stephen would be home in less than two hours. She wanted to have dinner ready so she could get back to the correspondence after they talked.

The entire day had been behind schedule. She'd overslept, Dr. Lee had been late, and now this. Genny grabbed her purse and rushed toward the store. Walking the aisles reminded her of the times she'd done the same for John. She had planned special menus for every night. The well-thumbed cookbooks were the result of her refusal to settle for the ordinary. John's enthusiastic praise of her culinary skills had been embarrassing at times. Maybe food was the way to a man's heart, but she had no idea what Stephen liked.

Everything took longer than expected—a trainee cashier, unpriced items, even an accident delay on the trip home. Stephen arrived home to find her in a state. "I'll get dinner started. The groceries are all over the kitchen, and I have to work on the mail tonight. I haven't done any work today."

"Honey, it's okay." He slipped a hand behind her neck and pulled her forward, placing a kiss on her forehead.

Stephen sat down, using one booted foot to push at the back of the other. The worn leather boot refused to move. "Don't know why I wear these things."

"Let me." The shoe didn't budge with her ineffectual tugs.

"It's easier if you straddle my leg."

Stepping into place, Genny turned her back to him and grabbed the boot, jerking it free. The other shoe followed. Before she straightened up, Stephen toppled her into his lap, his breath warm against her neck as he whispered, "Thanks."

Genny stiffened and scrambled to the far end of the sofa. The situation was entirely too cozy.

"What's got you so uptight? Your boss isn't going to yell at you because you're running behind schedule, you know."

Gas logs burned in the fireplace between the kitchen and sitting room. The flames flickered with merry abandonment generating a warmth that combined with her own heat to make her more uncomfortable. "I know."

Stephen stretched his long legs before him and wriggled his stockinged feet. "Then what's wrong?"

"I'm not very practiced in relationship games."

Her reluctant admittance brought a smile to his face. "Is that what this is?"

The heat skyrocketed to her brain, her cheeks heating even more as Genny considered her naïveté. How could she even suggest anything more?

His fingers closed about her hand, bringing it to his lips. "Not that I'm adverse to playing games with you."

A warning flag shot up. The two of them couldn't be alone in a room for ten minutes before awareness overpowered them.

"I spent a lot of time thinking this last trip." He propped his hands behind his head, a contented smile on his face. "I figured out why I'm thirty and unmarried."

"You mean a reason other than the fact that you're gorgeous

and popular with the women and have the lifestyle every man wants. . ." Genny broke off at his obvious enjoyment.

"Go on," he coaxed. "I love having my ego stroked as much as the next man."

A cranberry has nothing on me colorwise. Genny felt the blood rush upward. "You don't need it."

"Sure, I need to hear the woman I care about tell me I'm gorgeous. It's the only time the words really mean something."

"You've heard them before," she stammered.

"Not from a woman with impact."

"Impact?"

"I always knew the right woman would make me feel something. I never guessed it would be like driving my car into a brick wall." Stephen pounded his fist into his open hand. "Impact!"

He slid closer, bringing them together. "I've decided it's because I need an older woman. You."

Her view of the fire was replaced by Stephen's face as he kissed her.

Nervousness flooded through Genny. "Stephen?"

He sighed heavily. "I'm a grown man, Honey. I haven't been a little boy or an indecisive teenager in years. Once I make up make up my mind, it's full speed ahead."

"I know," Genny said, feeling unhappy with herself. Being with him contradicted every decision she'd made during his absence.

"You got something against May-December relationships?"

"December?" Genny sputtered. "I wouldn't go that far. I'm more of a late June, early July."

He chuckled at her indignant response. "I'm no spring chicken either."

Genny flashed him a derisive smile. "Yeah, you're getting older by the minute."

Stephen grinned. "All quality things improve with age."

Genny's hands went to his cheeks, holding him in place as she whispered, "I need you to be gloriously happy, Stephen.

I don't want you to look back with regrets."

"I don't want to look back. I want to look ahead to the future. A future with you and Jonathan." Genny felt completely wretched. "Don't give me that look. Why don't we discuss it over a candlelit dinner?"

"No." She needed to get away before she did something really stupid. "I have to work tonight."

"Then we'll stay in. I don't want to go out anyway. Too cold."

"The letters. . . I'll go back to the guesthouse."

Stephen stood. "Stay. Keep me company while I cook. I'd like to hear what you think of my fan mail."

So much for putting distance between them. "And I'd like to know about all the baby stuff that arrived. Hundreds of dollars worth of things I can't afford."

First confusion and then determination highlighted his features. "I didn't."

Genny glared at him. "I'll buy the things Jonathan needs as soon as I can."

"Listen to me. I didn't do it. I told my parents about you and Jonathan. They think. . . Well, anyway, my sister was there, and she got excited about Jonathan. Said she had all this baby stuff taking up space, and the next thing I knew she planned to ship it to you. What could I say?"

Genny closed her eyes. "Don't tell me. You come from a long line of overly generous people."

He shrugged. "We can't help it. Besides, what's wrong with having the things he needs without having to buy them? You can save the money for more important stuff."

More important stuff, Genny thought with a pang. *Like getting out of his life.* "I'll get the letters."

Anything Stephen had to say was forgotten when one of the grocery bags toppled. Genny slipped out the door as he moved to retrieve the items.

Grabbing the stack of letters she needed help with, Genny settled at the island and found herself watching Stephen. He looked so comfortable in the kitchen. Stephen bent to look in the fridge, and she forced her attention to the letters.

"Stir-fry okay?" At her nod, he piled the makings on the countertop. His system was fascinating. The letters lay untouched as he wielded the knife with cheflike precision, cutting scraped carrots into precise, dime thin slices. He reached for a green pepper. "So, what about the letters?"

"Mostly like you said. Requests for autographed pictures, free tickets, and contributions. Does Ray get as much mail as you?"

"Probably more. He's more outgoing with the fans."

"More outgoing? I can't imagine that. I'd say the ladies really like you handsome, single guys."

"Harper will die when we get married."

Genny felt a sinking feeling in her stomach. "There's some of it, well, one letter that's. . ." She cleared her throat. "Rather personal."

Stephen glanced at her. "What did it say?"

She thumbed through the stack of envelopes, finding the pink one. Its heavy scent permeated the room.

He laid down the knife and wiped his hands before slipping the letter from the envelope. His nose wrinkled. "Think she buys this stuff by the gallon?"

Genny thought more along the lines of industrial-sized drums. "It's pretty strong."

He scanned it, laughing outright as he crushed the flowery stationery into a ball and aimed it at the trash can. As he caught sight of her expression, he cried, "You didn't. . . You think I'm interested in what she described?"

"It's none of my business."

"Let me assure you, my woman would never write me letters describing what we do in private. This woman is probably one of those people who sell those incredible lies to the tabloids." Disgust etched lines of disapproval on his unsmiling face.

"It's none of my business," she repeated.

Stephen took her face in his hands. "Have you heard anything I've said to you?"

Genny attempted to draw a reviving breath as she nodded

slowly. Her heart had done flip-flops from the moment of his arrival, but nothing had changed. He was her friend, her employer, nothing more.

"Apparently I listen as well as you," she managed. "Sure, we're old enough to make our own decisions, mistakes even. But you've forgotten how having us around will change your life. I don't think it's such a good idea for me to live here."

His expression grew serious. "I thought we were past that."

"You deserve a spotlight woman. Not a plain-Jane."

"No, thanks." He looked as if the idea left a bad taste in his mouth. "You think people will wonder what I see in you?" She nodded agreement. "Let me tell you something, Genny. Some beauty doesn't go as deep as the skin. True beauty goes a lot deeper and lasts a lot longer. Think about that the next time you look in the mirror. You're too special to forget it."

Stephen walked out of the kitchen, and Genny fought the urge to call him back, to admit she didn't understand what was happening between them.

He returned, carrying a small box. "If you insist on gilding the lily, try this. Go on. Open it."

The beautifully wrapped package made a mockery of everything they had discussed.

"No." She pushed it back at him.

Stephen ripped away the paper. As Genny watched, he removed the lid. "Take it out," he encouraged, holding the ring box aloft when she made no move to do so. He popped the box lid open.

The emerald ring was the most beautiful thing she had ever seen.

"It's the same color as your eyes," Stephen said, tracing the stone with his finger. "I was walking down the street and saw it in a window. Ray thought it was hilarious that I had to go in and buy it."

She shook her head and tried to back away. "There are things you don't know."

He grasped her hands firmly. "I can't know if you won't tell me. I've listened to the protests, the arguments that I need someone you consider more suited. I'm not interested in a wife who's a vehicle for my career. I need a woman with a heart. With love to give. Those few years you argue about aren't important. Share your beauty with me, Genny. I need it badly."

Stephen pulled her into his arms. Genny wallowed in his tenderness, feeling no doubt the angels had truly been watching over her when they had sent him.

"Genny, what would you say if I asked you to marry me?"

thirteen

"I can't."

"Why? Because I'm a musician? Would you say yes if I had a nine-to-five job and reported home every night?"

Genny gasped. "No. Music's your life. Your wife should be young and beautiful, sophisticated enough to entertain the people you need to impress, an asset to your career. A woman who can give you children when you're ready for them."

"You seem to have everything figured out. There's only one problem. I love you. I am not looking for a beauty contestant to hang on my arm for the world to admire. You and Jonathan have become my family. When I'm away from you, I'm counting the moments until I'm home again."

"Please don't say that," Genny protested. As her feelings for him increased, it became more difficult to share the pathetic story of her life.

Heartfelt words poured from his mouth. "Do you have any idea what coming home to you means to me? It's like nothing I've ever known, and frankly I never want to be without it again."

"I thought you understood my need for independence."

"I'm not trying to take anything away from you."

"You're not making me reach for it either," she said, busily stacking the letters. "I can't even provide a home for my son. What kind of mother does that make me?"

"You're a wonderful mother."

"Not as long as I depend on others to provide my every need. How can I take care of Jonathan when I can't take care of myself?"

"If this is about money, I can place a lump sum in your account."

There was an audible sigh as she turned away from him. "Forget it, Stephen. You don't understand."

His hand rested on her shoulder. "I want to take care of you and Jonathan."

"Our relationship is too one-sided. You give and I take. That's not my style."

"But I love you."

Tormented by the confusing roller-coaster highs and lows of her emotions, Genny knew she had to confront this truthfully. "And I love you."

"Why do I have the feeling there's a 'but' to this?"

"Because I don't like feeling incompetent. I won't accept anyone feeling obligated to care for me or Jonathan. If you love me, you'll understand. I will control my destiny."

❧

Sleep was impossible. Stephen tossed aside the covers and left the bed. His mind raced with Genny's revelation. He'd learned more about her in that short discussion than in all the weeks he'd known her.

He walked to the French doors and stood watching the full moon, feeling the cold that made his warm breath fog the glass.

Did she resent the gifts? He liked doing special things for her and Jonathan. What other reason was there to work so hard? He gave a good percentage of his earnings to the ministry and had enough left over to live comfortably.

No doubt Genny had worked equally hard in her role as homemaker only to end up impoverished. Where did God fit into her plan to control her destiny? Did she honestly think she could depend on no one but herself?

Within hours, he would be on a bus headed for destinations that only took him out of her life. How could he gain Genny's trust when he stayed on the road so much?

Taking care of each other was mutual for a husband and wife. He would be as dependent on her as she was him. He couldn't be happy without the shared love and caring of the person who mattered most in the world to him.

A half hour ticked slowly by before Stephen gave up and went in search of sheet music for the song he needed to rehearse.

It wasn't in the file tray or on the desktop. He walked over to the table Genny used for work. Maybe I should have her organize my sheet music, he thought as he checked the neat area. He slid the center drawer open and stared down at the landscaping plan.

Eager eyes quickly assessed the drawing. It was his house, complete with a six-foot brick privacy fence and water feature, and so much more. So many of his ideas, thoughts he had never gotten around to putting on paper, were there.

Genny had taken the things they discussed the night they discovered a shared love of gardening and incorporated them into this plan to beautify his home. She had a gift.

The realization struck him. Quite possibly the answer to their dilemma. When he got back, he intended to prove how much he loved her. It was time for Genny to get on with her life, to be as happy as he knew she could be.

Stephen kneeled by the desk. "Father, I come to You with a request that You guide Genny and me to what You would have for us. I feel so happy when I'm with her, so confident she's the one. I know her life has not been easy. Help her realize she can't do it alone. Bring her back to Your loving arms. Amen."

❧

Genny's lethargy tempted her to stay in bed the next morning. She only wanted to hide from the fervent desire to say yes to Stephen's proposal.

Without bothering to check, Genny knew the bus had left earlier, headed for points unknown. Already she missed him terribly. Her unrest disturbed Genny. For years she'd been happy as John's wife. Or had she?

Genny suspected her need to feel loved after the nightmarish way things turned out played an even bigger part in her happiness. Determination that her marriage not be like her parents' kept her going when times got hard.

What would be so different with Stephen? The question bounced around inside her head. He was the most wonderful man she'd ever known. She should be so happy. Instead uncertainties that refused to go away filled her.

His solution of putting money in her account bothered Genny. She knew he cared and only thought of her and Jonathan. If she needed tangible proof, all she had to do was look at the gifts he gave her. "Things," she whispered almost disdainfully. And just as suddenly Genny realized she only wanted his love.

The thought stayed with her throughout the day. Work, Jonathan, nothing took her mind off the truth. The phone rang late that night.

"Hi, Hon," Stephen said tentatively, sounding almost afraid she wouldn't talk to him.

Laughter filled the background. Who owns the high-pitched feminine one? Genny wondered. "Sounds like a party."

"The guys are giving Denise a hard time. How are you? And Jonathan?"

Denise Wilson, Genny realized, not liking the surge of jealousy. The beautiful singer accompanied them on the tour and opened for the band. "Fine."

"Can we talk about last night?"

She steeled herself for the dreaded confrontation. "I wasn't exactly myself."

"Yes, you were. You opened up to me about your needs. I couldn't sleep so I went into the study and found the landscaping plans."

Genny frowned. She had intended to bring them over to the guesthouse. "I wanted to surprise you."

"They're sensational. You put the dreams I had the first time I walked the property on paper. Things I've never told another living soul."

The design had incorporated most of her personal preferences. "It's not finished."

"I figured I'd have to hire a landscaping firm. When I saw

your plan, I thought why not you? I know it's winter but you could collect plants, grow some in the greenhouse, and hire contractors to start the fence. You could have a reputable landscape design business going in no time."

Stephen couldn't know that for years she had dreamed of going into business for herself. She had landscaped the yard of her home, turning it into a veritable showplace.

After their discussion, Genny filled a number of solitary hours formulating the plan for his grounds. For fun. She never actually considered doing the work. "Reputable businesses require operating capital," Genny pointed out.

"I'd give you a loan. On paper, with interest and everything."

The woman's high-pitched giggle ran down Genny's spine like nails on a chalkboard. She wanted to scream when Denise distracted Stephen with her pleas to make them stop.

"You'd better get back to the fun and games."

"Ah, Gen, don't go. I waited all day to talk to you."

Just as she'd waited to hear his voice. Genny didn't want to doubt Stephen. No more than she had John. She knew nothing about Stephen's ability to resist a beautiful woman, but she couldn't hold a candle to Denise Wilson.

"We'll discuss this when you get home. Have fun."

"Genny, wait, please. Let me go to another room so we can talk."

Background chatter and then Stephen's yell for them to hang up sounded over the phone. "Okay, that's better. I'm not trying to push you into anything. Just offering options."

Genny giggled. "You making me an offer I can't refuse?"

Laughter relieved the tension. "I'd love to hear you say yes."

The giggle evolved into a sigh. "Oh, Stephen, every offer you make tempts me to the point where I don't even want to think about what the future holds. I can't allow that to happen."

"You're right."

His words shocked her. She blinked and waited for more.

"You need to consider the future with prayer. How's Jonathan today?"

Change the topic. That worked for her. "Wonderful as usual. His doctor says he'll release him soon if he continues to improve. I can't wait to get him home. I have plans to spoil him rotten."

"Sounds like he'll need a father figure to temper all that loving."

Genny shook her head at his obvious ploy. She changed the subject again. "You don't need to pay anyone to do the grounds work. Digging in the earth relaxes me. I've already been in your greenhouse. I planted several packets of seeds I found in a box in the pantry. I dug through the bulbs too. Some should have gone in before Christmas but there were a few that will bloom if I plant them now. I can do that if you tell me where you want them."

"Where ever you think best. I have no idea. I keep a lot of gardening catalogs on the bus and order things I like. A lot of stuff never gets planted. They rolled the sod in the front yard or I'd have weeds. There's stuff in the barn too. Statuary, yard doodads, a fountain."

Poor Stephen. His sacrifice was evident in his regret-filled tone. "Don't you ever get a vacation?"

"When I fight for time off. As a matter of fact, I told Chuck I'm taking a couple of weeks when they release Jonathan from the hospital."

A red flag popped up in Genny's head. Why would he choose Jonathan's release to take time off?

"I thought I could help you get settled in and spend a bit of time with my namesake. What do you think?"

What did she think? "If it's what you want."

"I can't think of anything I'd like better. I've got to go. The guys want to run through the new song again tonight. I'll talk to you tomorrow. Love you."

"Have a good session." Genny replaced the receiver, barely able to swallow past the lump in her throat. She loved Stephen Camden, more than she'd ever loved anyone, but the demon she fought was fear. Panic that she wouldn't be woman enough for the man of her dreams. And this time, it would be much more difficult to survive if she lost him.

The days dragged on. Stephen called several times but they avoided certain topics. Genny frequently made excuses to get off the phone, and by Friday, she felt edgy. Good news came in the form of Jonathan's imminent release from the hospital.

"When will you bring him home?" Stephen asked that night.

"His pediatrician is thinking next week. I'm excited but afraid. He's so tiny."

"Honey, you'll do great. You'll be able to make up for lost time. Jonathan's going to know so much love. How about I go with you to pick him up?"

"I'd like that."

There was satisfaction in his tone as he said, "So would I. And no more worrying. It causes wrinkles."

Genny laughed and agreed, "Something I can't afford at my great old age."

"You're not old."

"I'm on the downhill slide toward forty. Let's see how you feel in a few years when you start the trek."

"You've got Jonathan to keep you young, Beautiful."

Beautiful. Though she knew it wasn't true, the one word lifted her spirits immeasurably. "Bye, Stephen. Take care."

fourteen

Are you okay?" Stephen asked, surprised to find Genny wearing her robe when she opened the door. He glanced at his watch. It was Thursday. The day Jonathan came home. He'd caught a flight home so he could go to the hospital with her. "I was sure you'd be too excited to sleep."

Genny covered a yawn and gestured him inside. "Welcome home." She stumbled into the sitting area and dropped onto the sofa. Her head rested against the arm, traitorous eyes closing against her will.

"Genny?" Stephen called, shaking her. "What's wrong?"

"Tired," she said, her eyes closing again.

"Didn't you sleep last night?"

"When Jonathan would let me."

He leaned over her inert form. "Jonathan? Is he all right?" he demanded anxiously.

Her face came alive with the brilliant but sleepy smile. "He came home yesterday. I spent the night adjusting to motherhood. Those early morning feedings are a joy. I woke up every time he so much as moved in the bassinet. They told me it would be like that, but I never realized. . ." Another yawn escaped.

Stephen was disappointed. "But you said today."

"I wasn't going to say no when Dr. Lee said he could come home yesterday." Genny rose from the sofa and walked toward the kitchenette. "Coffee?"

He followed, climbing onto a bar stool.

In minutes, she had eggs sizzling and bread in the toaster. Somewhere along the way, she tuned the radio to a Christian station.

Angry cries filled the guesthouse. "That's my boy. He

might just be the most vocal roomie I've ever had." Genn
slapped the spatula into his hand. "Watch our breakfast."

Stephen smiled as she bustled away, all vestiges of h
exhaustion gone. He took plates from the cabinet, remove
the toast, and flipped the eggs.

She returned, cuddling the blanketed baby. "You fee
Jonathan. I'll finish breakfast."

"You bet," Stephen agreed, abandoning the kitchen chore
Eagerness turned to hesitation when she placed the tiny bun
dle in his arms. He tried to give him back. "He's too little. I
better cook."

Genny pulled Stephen's arm into place, tested the bottl
and helped him guide it into Jonathan's mouth. "He does a
the work. Just in case." She placed a cloth diaper over h
shoulder. "The fun job is burping him."

He liked the way Jonathan attacked the small bottle of fo
mula. The domesticity of the scene pleased him—Genny, st
in her favorite shabby bathrobe, making breakfast while I
fed the baby. He could handle more mornings like this.

Too soon, she slid a plate of food on the table. "I'll tal
over. Eat before your food gets cold."

Food had never held less appeal. "He's almost finished. H
eyes are closed, but watch his mouth when I try to take th
bottle away."

Big blue eyes popped open when Genny removed th
bottle. "I'll put him down and join you for breakfast."

Stephen shot to his feet. "I'll help."

❧

He led the way, watching as she settled the baby in the crib.
colorful mobile that matched the cartoon characters on th
bedding hung over the end of the crib. Stephen wound it u
Jonathan's eyes opened again. "A music lover already."

"Hand me that blanket."

She bundled Jonathan snugly.

"What are you doing? He can't move like that."

"We had an incident last night because I allowed him

et overstimulated. I was ready to take him back. Trina said
ne doctor wouldn't have allowed me to bring him home if he
adn't thought I could handle it."

Stephen touched her cheek, trailing his fingertips over the
oft skin. "I have no doubt that you can." He struggled to
ide his yawn.

Genny kissed his cheek, lingering as she breathed the deli-
ously male scents she associated with Stephen. "Someone
se needs a nap."

"The concert ended late, and I caught an early flight."

Genny's hand covered her mouth, her eyes widening with
ismay. "Oh, Stephen, I'm sorry. I should have called."

"It's okay. You managed fine. I'm proud of you."

☙

Genny refused to allow Jonathan's homecoming to stand in
ne way of her work. She dressed and straightened the kitchen.
tephen's obvious disappointment touched her deeply.

As for feeding Jonathan, once he became comfortable,
tephen hadn't wanted to let go. What was his fascination
ith her son?

Genny resisted the temptation to stand over the crib and
atch Jonathan sleep. She took the mail into the living room,
etting a monitor on the nearby end table. Stopping only
hen the baby woke for feedings, she managed to get
rough a pile of fan mail.

Stephen reappeared that afternoon, refreshed and even
nore eager to lend a hand. "What can I do to help?"

Genny settled on the sofa. A fire burned on the grate,
nocking the edge off their most recent cold snap.

He warmed his hands. "You think Jonathan's warm
nough? It's raining. I wouldn't be surprised if it turns to ice."

"Rule of thumb is he's comfortable when we are. Besides,
ne heat's on."

"It's still chilly."

Droplets of water glistened on Stephen's hair. "You're cold
ecause you just came in."

"So, how can I help?" he asked again.

"Jonathan will probably want his dinner shortly. Mea while, there are plenty of letters if you'd care to read a few."

He settled beside her, one long arm trailing along the ba of the sofa. Genny glanced at him, noting the intensity his gaze.

"So have you given any more consideration to what I ask before I left?" Her face felt frozen as she tried to smile a nod. "And did you notice I've behaved myself and have pushed?" Genny nodded again. "And wouldn't you say good boys deserve a reward?" This time he didn't wait for answer as he leaned over and kissed her.

At her whispered protest, Stephen pulled her into a h "Just let me hold you."

There in his arms, Genny forgot the doubts, the prese the past, the future.

The moment both realized the temptation they faced, tl moved apart. Genny reclined at the opposite end of the sc encouraging him to talk about his trip. She shared a couple requests she found particularly touching.

Jonathan's cries brought them to their feet. Together, tl moved to the small nursery.

"Hello, Darling," she cooed. "Look, Stephen, he's smiling "I'll be right back."

Genny looked after him, surprised by his sudden desertic The camera in his hand explained Stephen's absence. "H him up."

"Wouldn't it be better if we were dressed for picture-taking

"You look beautiful," he said. "Now, show me those smile

The camera clicked time after time before he replaced lens cap. He rewound the film and stuck the roll into pocket. Genny popped a pacifier into Jonathan's mouth. "Y know what you're doing with that."

Stephen returned the camera to its case. "It's a hobby. I got albums of pictures from places I've visited. If you want, find them for you."

"Yes, please. I'm an avid armchair traveler."

"I want you to keep this." He set the camera on the bed. "Start an album for Jonathan. I'll miss a lot of his growing up while I'm on tour so I'd like to have the pictures, or maybe I should get a video camera?"

She laid Jonathan on the changing table. "Don't you take it with you?"

"I have a couple."

"I'll try, but don't expect too much."

He moved closer and slipped a finger in Jonathan's hand. "I'll show your mommy some of the tips I've picked up so she gets great pictures of you for me."

"That would help." Genny pulled Jonathan's clothing back in place and lifted him to her shoulder. "You want to hold him?"

"You don't mind?"

Stephen seemed surprised by the offer. She commended herself on her remarkable restraint. She would make the sacrifice. After all, she would have many hours to cuddle her child. "If you baby-sit, I can finish the letters."

Jonathan rested on Stephen's knees, his blanket unwrapped as Stephen studied him like a proud parent. "You're a miracle, little guy. Did you know that?" He spoke softly to the baby. "Look at this tiny hand." He grinned broadly when Jonathan wrapped his silver-dollar-sized hand about his thumb. "That's some grip, Buddy. Want to arm wrestle?"

Genny smiled at Stephen's teasing. It was difficult to concentrate. She wanted to be part of the fun, not a bystander.

Genny stopped work frequently when Stephen insisted she see what Jonathan was doing. She finally gave up and joined them on the sofa. Once Jonathan had been fed and put to bed, Stephen suggested, "Why don't I fix us something? We can eat in front of the fire."

"I'll help."

Hunger or happiness gave her appetite the edge to consume her portion of the food they prepared. She leaned against the corner of the sofa.

Stephen eyed her speculatively and slid closer. "Why are you sitting all the way down there? Don't you trust yourself around me?"

Genny laughed and tapped his arm playfully. "Behave."

He shrugged and frowned. "I'm trying to be patient. You should know I'm not known for my patience."

"Duly noted," Genny said with a nod. "And you should know I rarely waver in the decision-making process as much as I have recently."

"Oh, I almost forgot," Stephen said. "Ray wants you to handle his mail. I told him what a relief it was not to have to deal with it. He says maybe I'll be able to find time for some of the things I'm always complaining I never have time to do."

The conversation turned to the activity of the week. Both were surprised to find the evening had slipped past.

"We should call it a night." Together they stacked plates on the tray. "I'll get you a refrigerator for the nursery tomorrow."

"A what?" Genny looked at him curiously. What on earth was he talking about?

"Refrigerator. One of those small ones. They don't take much room."

Genny found the extravagant gesture humorous. "It's twenty steps to the kitchen, Stephen."

"I don't want you stumbling about in the middle of the night."

"Why not a baby nurse to bring Jonathan to me in bed? I'm teasing!" Genny said before he could offer. "Did I ever tell you you're a sweet, sweet man?"

"Yes, but I don't mind hearing it again."

He kissed her good night. After he left, the night was pretty much a repeat of the one before, except that Genny lay awake a bit longer, thinking how much she enjoyed Stephen's company.

Jonathan's cries stirred her in the early hours. She flipped on the bedside lamp, and lifted her son from the bassinet. Detouring by the kitchen, she placed a bottle in the warmer, and carried him into the tiny nursery for a diaper change.

The baby refused to be contented. Had he experienced the same spells while in the hospital? She walked the small space in hopes of calming him down. She was beside herself when there was a knock on the door.

"Genny? Is everything okay?" Stephen asked when she let him in. "I was in the study and saw the lights." Stephen smoothed a hand over Jonathan's head. "What's wrong with my little buddy? May I?"

She readily placed the bundled infant into his arms, feeling even more insecure that she couldn't comfort her son. Stephen headed for the nursery rocker.

"Poor baby." Genny knelt by the chair, her fingers smoothing the dark, thick curls. Stephen offered the bottle she attempted minutes before, and this time Jonathan ate.

"You want to feed him?"

She shook her head and leaned back on her heels to watch them together.

The clock John gave her for their tenth anniversary marked the passing of time with a little tune.

Jonathan lingered over the bottle, flailing his tiny fists in the air now and then. "You think he doesn't realize it's dark outside?"

"At least he stopped screaming. Why don't you sing him a lullaby? Heaven only knows, the poor babe isn't going to learn music appreciation from me," Genny prompted when Stephen balked.

Stephen tucked the infant against his shoulder and set the rocker in motion. One big hand softly caressed Jonathan's back. A big burp combined with the soft timbre of his voice, and they both grinned.

Genny sighed in pure delight as he finished the song. "That was beautiful," she whispered, trailing Stephen as he returned the sleeping infant to the bassinet. "Yours?"

"An original unpublished Camden." He pressed a warning finger to his lips when Jonathan stirred.

After checking the blanket and flipping the lamp off, Genny followed him into the kitchenette. "Why haven't you released it?"

"Some things are private."

Silence filled the room. Smothering a groan, Stephen stepped closer to Genny. "That didn't come out right. When I first started, I played in dives and beat the paths, hoping for success for the better part of ten years. I made a living but I was an unknown getting nowhere fast.

"I'd made up my mind to quit when Ray and the others wanted to form the band. Cowboy Jamboree caught on quickly, and we've managed to stay in the charts. Things changed after the CMA Horizon nomination. It's been a long hard pull, but I'd say it's been well worth the effort.

"But recently I've found the realization of one dream leaves room for another to take its place. I wrote that lullaby on our last road trip. For the child I'd like to consider my son. I promised not to push, but I want a family—you and Jonathan. Please give me some hope. Say you're considering my proposal."

Genny looked into his eyes, feeling the same yearning she saw in the stormy gray depths. "Yes, Stephen, I am. And I'm not taking the situation lightly," she admitted. "You hold a very special place in my heart."

Stephen gathered her into his arms and kissed her. "You are my heart," he whispered.

❧

The same weary mother greeted Stephen early the next morning. "How about I take young Jonathan over to the house while you shower and dress?"

Genny yawned widely. Between Jonathan's feedings and their late-night chat, she'd been awake half the night. "Has it stopped raining?"

"Yeah, the sun's struggling to break through."

"Let me bundle him up and heat a bottle."

Genny showered and dressed in a pair of old jeans and a shirt. Even though Jonathan had been home only a couple of nights, the place seemed quiet in his absence. She eyed the bed for a moment longer, tempted to crawl back in and pull the covers over her head until she had an answer.

No sense hiding. Stephen wouldn't allow her to do it for long anyway. How she wished she could give him the answer he wanted, but she couldn't say yes. Not yet. Maybe never. And it wasn't fair to ask him to wait.

She stopped in his kitchen to pour herself a mug of coffee before following Stephen's voice to the study. At first, she thought he must be on the phone. Affection filled her as Genny found them in Stephen's recliner, Jonathan propped against his chest as he read aloud from the newspaper. "Can you believe that?"

Genny laughed out loud at Stephen's incredulous inquiry. "He has some pretty interesting reactions to the state of the world, don't you think?"

Stephen laughed as he glanced down at the baby. "Our Jonathan here is a man of few words. I thought you might have decided to sleep in."

"The brain's willing but my internal alarm went off. There's too much to do." Genny smoothed a loving hand over the baby's head. She glanced up and found herself startled by the open longing in Stephen's eyes. She couldn't get his late-night words off her mind. "I'm tired, but I need to get on those letters."

"You don't have to work all the time, Genny. Another day or so isn't going to make a difference."

"Tomorrow will bring a bring a new batch."

Stephen shrugged. "Keep the evening free. Ray's coming over, and we're going out."

"I can't," she protested.

"Sure you can. It's all arranged."

She stiffened at his assumption. "I don't appreciate having plans dropped on me after they're finalized."

"Nothing's changed, has it, Gen?"

How could he ask that? They had crossed the boundary to

admitted love for each other, and there was no going back to the comfort of friendship. Doubts shafted through her like the sharp blade of a freshly honed knife. "Everything's changed, Stephen."

"I haven't. You're just as precious to me. My feelings have deepened, but they haven't changed. I'll work harder to prove it if you force me to, but I won't give up. As for the plans, this event came up, and I thought you might like to go with us. I knew you'd need a baby-sitter, so I asked the guys. Slay volunteered. Said Ronnie would help him."

Genny envisioned leaving her son alone with two strange men and immediately rejected the idea.

"Jonathan will love Ronnie. She's Slay's wife," Stephen explained, not giving Genny an opportunity to refuse.

"Ronnie? What kind of name is that?"

"Actually she's Veronica. Randy Slayman is our keyboard player."

"How many children do they have?" she asked suspiciously.

"They're expecting their first," he admitted with a sheepish grin. "They could use the experience."

"And you expect me to allow them to practice with my son?"

Stephen folded the paper and laid it aside. "They're intelligent, qualified adults. I think you like arguing with me."

Horror made her hands tremble to the point where she slopped coffee over the side of the mug as she set it on the table. "No."

"Genny? What is it? I was only teasing."

"I hate arguing. And I'm afraid to leave him. What if something happened? I'd never forgive myself."

"You can't be with him around-the-clock until he's off to college," Stephen reasoned. "We'd only be gone for three hours or so."

"I'll think about it."

"Do that. You're more than Jonathan's mom. Leaving him now and again will do you more good than you realize."

"Maybe." More than Jonathan's mom. Who was she?

Daughter, sister, wife, widow, and mother. These were her roles in life. She didn't know how to be anyone else, particularly Stephen Camden's romantic interest. "I think I'll skip breakfast. I'm not really hungry."

"You're not a child."

"Interesting observation," Genny said. "Let me take Jonathan so you can finish your paper in peace."

"I'll bring him home after we cover the local news." He nodded toward the desk. "I noticed the photos. Did you need some signed?"

"It can wait. You should rest."

"Signing my name a couple hundred times isn't exactly strenuous work."

"Why don't you pursue some of those other interests you mentioned last night?"

A mischievous grin touched his face. "Because the interest I want to pursue isn't agreeable."

Genny's chest felt as if it would burst. She couldn't help but feel flattered by this man's attention.

"I promise to look and not touch," he said softly, the gray gaze holding hers. "For now."

The remainder of the day passed in a flash and by the time they finished an early dinner, Ray was at the door. Stephen showed him into the living room where Genny nervously awaited the arrival of the baby-sitters.

Ray sat beside her, admiring Jonathan. "Where are Ronnie and Slay? I thought they'd be here by now."

"He called about fifteen minutes ago," Stephen said. "They're on their way."

"What sort of benefit is this?" Genny asked Ray.

Stephen's hands rested on her shoulders. "Oh, no you don't. It's a surprise."

"Ray, tell me," she coaxed.

He glanced at Genny and then at Stephen. "Keep her guessing, Ray."

"Come on, guys. Tell me. Please."

"No way. You'll need your jacket. It's chilly out."

"Oh, it's at the cleaners," Genny said. "Jonathan spit up on me. I told you it wasn't practical. I guess I can't go."

"Hon, you're not getting off that easily. Let Ray hold Jonathan and come with me." When she hesitated, Stephen said, "Can't you see he's dying to get his hands on that boy?"

She settled her son in Ray's arms and watched to make sure he was comfortable. "I'll be right back."

Stephen pulled her to the hall coat closet. Genny watched as he rifled through the hangers.

"Aren't we going to be inside?"

He grinned and flashed her another "I'm not telling" look. She sighed her exasperation. He was much too good at this game.

Stephen pulled a coat from the closet. "Try this."

The fur-lined jacket was large but fit well enough. She pulled the lapels into place, breathing in the odor of fine leather. The sleeves fell over her hands when she dropped her arms to her sides.

Stephen adjusted the snaps on the cuffs to improve the fit. "Have you got gloves? A hat?"

"And a scarf," she added. "Cashmere. Sonya gave them to me last Christmas."

"A coat would have been better."

The aggrieved look she flashed him spoke volumes. The doorbell chimed, and Stephen reached to open the door, introducing the new arrivals to Genny.

Within minutes, Genny knew she could trust the Slaymans with her son. "He's been fed and is asleep. Chances are he won't wake. The doctor's number is on the desk by the phone." She glanced at Stephen and back to Ronnie. "Mr. Secretive here better give you the emergency number since he won't tell me where we're going."

"Slay has my cell number," Stephen said, dropping her scarf about her neck. "But he's not going to need it. Right, Slay?"

"Right, Steve," he agreed happily. "I hope you're wrong

about Jonathan sleeping the entire time. We hoped for the opportunity to play with your little guy."

Fresh worries came at the thought of Jonathan's crying spells. "He was a preemie, so you have to be careful not to get him overexcited. If he starts to cry. . ."

"Don't worry, Genny," Ronnie assured. "My sister's baby was premature." Ronnie smiled at her husband and balanced one hand on her extended stomach. "Slay thinks he can master the art in one evening of baby-sitting. Of course, I've told him I know it all. I'm the oldest of seven children and an experienced aunt. Go and enjoy the surprise."

With every step, Genny forced back the unease and allowed herself to be escorted to Ray's four-wheel drive vehicle. Stephen gave her a gentle boost into the high cab. She glanced at the stick shift and back at him.

"Looks like you'll have to sit in my lap."

Genny inched closer to Ray, latched the center seat belt, and cinched it up.

Grinning, Stephen latched his seat belt then dropped an arm about her shoulders, pulling her up against his chest. "Dance with the one who brung you," he murmured in her ear.

"Considering I have two dates," she emphasized, "that could be difficult."

The lights from an oncoming vehicle gave her a glimpse of his smile. "You're with me. Always."

"Tell me where we're going," she wheedled shamelessly.

"Wait and see," he persisted.

Her questions were answered with their arrival at the county fairgrounds. She had read about the benefit rodeo in the paper a couple of days before. "We can't go in there. You'll be mobbed."

Stephen slid from the cab and lifted his arms to catch her. "Sure we can."

Genny moved toward him, her gaze stopping on a mother and baby crossing the parking lot.

"He'll be okay, Honey," Stephen whispered, setting her on

her feet and linking her fingers in his. "I promise. Do you think I'd let anything happen to Jonathan? I love him too."

They went through a private entrance, escaping the worst of the crowd. People were everywhere, and Genny's gaze darted about, certain they would be mobbed the moment someone recognized Stephen or Ray.

When no one seemed to notice, Genny decided she was being paranoid. Still she felt relieved when Stephen helped her into the roped-off bleachers facing the arena.

"I've never been to a rodeo before."

"You'll enjoy yourself," he promised, snapping her jacket and tucking the scarf closer about her neck. "Warm enough?"

"Yes, Daddy."

Stephen grinned and slipped an arm about her waist.

For the next couple of hours, Genny enjoyed herself tremendously. Stephen and Ray were introduced and spoke briefly on the importance of the fund-raiser, encouraging people to dig deeper in their pockets. Riders and mounts paraded around the arena as one event followed another.

Genny enjoyed the horsemanship of the barrel racers and the calf dogging, but the clowns' sidesplitting antics brought tears of mirth to her eyes.

One by one, horses charged from the chutes, their riders holding on with all their might as the horse bucked and twisted in its determination to eject them. One cowboy got his foot hung up in the wild mount's stirrup. Unable to watch, Genny gasped and buried her face in Stephen's chest.

He massaged her shoulder tenderly. "Don't worry, Love. These guys are tough. See, the pickup men got him."

Genny trembled with relief as the two men rode from the arena. The last rider won the purse, staying on for what Genny considered the longest seconds she'd ever lived through. A grin split the cowboy's face when he jumped to the ground and waved his hat in the air.

The loudspeaker came to life. "Ladies and gents, this unlucky cowboy drew the biggest, meanest bull this side of

Texas. Let's hear it for Joe Kincaid riding Torture Time."

Animal and rider charged from the stall. The white hat was the first thing to go as the wily animal tossed his rider to and fro like a rag doll in a windstorm.

"Ouch," she muttered when he went down. The clowns rushed out to divert the bull's attention and the raging monster ran off. When the animal charged the fence in front of them, Genny shifted, sure she felt his powerful snort before he turned away.

"These guys are crazy," she whispered to Stephen.

"They're definitely braver than me. Had enough?" Stephen asked a few minutes later.

"I'm freezing," she admitted.

"Why didn't you say so?" He leaned over her to speak to Ray, and she stared at his expressive face, thinking how much she enjoyed looking at Stephen. Their eyes met, his eyebrows lifting. She smiled and dropped her gaze to her hands.

"Let's go." They slipped off the end of the bleachers and moved toward the exit.

"Hey, there's Stephen Camden and Ray Marshall," a woman yelled. Genny withdrew as the group converged on them.

A teenage girl thrust a piece of paper at Stephen. "Can I have your autograph?"

Genny watched as he charmed them with words and actions, jealousy sweeping over her when another woman attached herself to his arm. His warm smile set Genny's teeth on edge, and she stomped toward the truck, only to wait several minutes longer for Ray to unlock the door.

"Wow," he breathed, "that was some crowd. Poor Stephen hasn't gotten away yet."

"Maybe poor Stephen doesn't want to get away," Genny snapped, struggling unaided into the cab.

"He can't help it if the fans like him."

"I didn't say he could. Besides, I thought you were the more outgoing one," Genny snapped.

Stephen's broad smile reflected in the glow of the interior

light as he dived into the truck. "Those fans were wilder than the rodeo cowboys," he declared. "Why did you disappear like that? I wanted to introduce you to the local fan club president."

"Please, those women only had eyes for you. Ray, will you turn the heat up? I'm freezing."

Stephen slipped an arm about her shoulders and drew her against his body. "It's only fair," he said when she squirmed in protest. "I kept you out in the cold for so long."

"What did you think of the rodeo?" Ray asked, filling the sudden lull in conversation.

"Maybe I could become a rodeo clown."

"Over my dead body," Stephen muttered.

"It could be arranged," Genny said as they faced off in the battle of wills. The house came into sight, effectively ending the argument.

"That looks like Sonya's car," Genny said, leaning forward for a closer look. "What's she doing here?"

"Why don't we find out?" Stephen suggested.

Lights blazed throughout the house. From the entrance hall, they heard copious weeping and Ronnie's agitated pleas. "Ms. Kelly, please calm down. You're frightening the baby."

Stephen hurried into the room, Genny on his heels. "What's going on here?"

Accusing eyes focused on Genny. "Where have you been?" Sonya demanded. "I needed you."

"The baby woke," Ronnie explained. "And then Ms. Kelly arrived. I haven't had time to feed him."

"Why don't you do it now?" Genny suggested, more than a little afraid Sonya would make a scene. "Where's Slay?"

"Making coffee."

"I'll help him," Ray volunteered.

Genny dropped onto the sofa beside her sister as the others left the room. Stephen remained nearby. "What on earth has happened?"

"My money," Sonya sobbed. "It's gone."

Genny gasped. "What?"

"I followed through on that tip I told you about. I lost everything."

Genny glanced at Stephen and back to Sonya as her arms slipped about her sister. "How could they take your money like that? Don't worry. Stephen will have his attorney check this out."

"How much?" Stephen asked.

"Twenty-five thousand." The words came out in a whimper.

Stephen emitted a shrill whistle.

"It's going to be okay," Genny said. "You've got your job."

Sonya sniffed. "There's no future for me there. I wanted to start my own firm."

Ray slid a tray onto the table and poured Sonya a cup of coffee.

"Genny, Slay and Ronnie probably could use a little help getting Jonathan settled," Stephen suggested.

His words prompted her to her feet. "How could that happen?" Genny asked as they walked into the kitchen. Slay held Jonathan.

"I see you got your wish," Genny said. "Ready to become a father?"

"More than ever."

"How was the rodeo?" Ronnie asked.

"It was fun. Thanks for making it possible."

"Our pleasure. We're sorry about the confusion. She arrived about a half hour ago. I tried to calm her down."

"I'm the one who's sorry," Genny said. "Sonya's high-strung."

"She kept talking about money. Is there anything we can do?" Slay asked.

Genny felt warmed by their concern. "Thanks. Stephen's checking into it for her."

Slay glanced down at the baby. "I think this little fellow is out for the count."

"He's such a sweetie," Ronnie added, touching Jonathan's head with loving fingers. "We want to take him home with us."

"Get your own," Stephen growled playfully.

Slay passed Jonathan to Genny and wrapped his arm about Ronnie. "We're working on it."

Everyone laughed. "We've got to get going," Slay said. "It past Ronnie's bedtime."

The woman flashed her husband a loving look. "He's goin to pamper me to death."

"What a lovely way to go," Genny said, swallowing hard a she realized that's exactly what Stephen was doing for her.

"I'll see them out and meet you in the study," Stephen sai "We need to talk."

Genny couldn't resist cuddling Jonathan. After verifying h was okay, she put him in his carrier, slipped off the jacket, an hung it in the closet before going in search of Stephen.

"You finally decided to come?" Stephen dropped the pe and stack of photos on the table. He took the carrier an placed Jonathan on the love seat.

"Can't this wait? I need to check on Sonya."

"Give me a couple of minutes. Please."

Genny sat on the sofa. "I'm not certain I want to hear thi Particularly if it's about my behavior. You didn't ask if wanted to go to the rodeo. You didn't ask how I felt abou Ronnie and Slay baby-sitting. Granted, everything worke out, but I prefer being asked."

"Point taken. What about that group of fans?"

"I felt. . .invisible."

Stephen rubbed a weary hand across his forehead. "I don see other women. There's only one whose image haunts m and I desire no one but her. You."

"I don't mean to hurt you, Stephen," Genny cried, droppin to her knees before him. She clutched his arms, forcing hir to lift his face and look at her. "I never want to hurt you."

He searched her face, wariness filling his eyes. "John's dea Genny." He silenced her with fingers against her lips. "H wouldn't begrudge you your happiness. I can make you happ Just don't fight me every step of the way."

"Stephen," she whispered as she faced the inevitable. Sh

oved him. If she kept herself from this special man, she would never again find such a love.

Genny rested her head against his chest, closing her eyes as she listened to the steady thump of his heart. Why had he made her love him?

"I'm an idiot," he whispered. "No sensible man would take a beautiful woman to a rodeo on a cold winter night. Not to mention invite a friend along. I should have taken you someplace special."

She lifted her head and looked at him. "But I liked the rodeo. And I like Ray. And the Slaymans too."

"You need romance. I need to woo you. Pamper you."

One soft, slender arm followed her hand across his body as she wrapped it about him, her next words spoken from the heart. "You already spoil me sinfully."

"If you'll let me, I'll treasure you."

fifteen

Genny needed to make a decision. Every time she saw t
longing in his gaze, she felt like an ice cream cone in the har
of a deprived child. She'd never known anyone so free w
compliments. Her self-esteem appreciated the boost.

"You know I've taken a couple of weeks off?"

Genny nodded. "I want to spend the time with you a
Jonathan. I know Sonya needs you, but promise you won't
her hurt you again."

"She won't."

"Will you think about what I've said?"

"I've done nothing but think, Stephen," she admitted. "Y
need to think too." Genny's heart was breaking as she said t
words. "You don't want to marry a thirty-six-year-old wom
with another man's child."

He surged forward, meeting her stubborn resistance w
his own. "Honey, if you believe that, you don't have a cl
about what I need."

Genny picked up the baby carrier and moved into the l
ing room. "Sonya, you can stay at the guesthouse with
You're in no condition to drive home."

They said good night and crossed the backyard. Af
putting Jonathan to bed, Genny fixed cocoa and listened
Sonya rant about the situation. Her levels of anger w
exhausting.

"Why don't we call it a night? I'm sure things will lo
better in the morning."

"I need something to sleep in," Sonya said, going to sear
through Genny's closet.

Genny removed a clean but worn nightgown from t
dresser drawer. "You can use this."

136

Sonya's nose wrinkled with distaste. She glanced around the room. "This place is really nice." Genny didn't say anything. "Where were you tonight?"

"Stephen took me to a benefit rodeo."

Sonya tossed the nightgown on the bed and sat, coiling her long legs beneath her. "The man obviously has a thing for you. Look at all he does."

"Our relationship isn't about what he can give me."

"So you admit there is a relationship?"

A flicker of apprehension coursed through Genny. She didn't want to share the truth with Sonya. She couldn't bear to have something as beautiful as their love made dirty by Sonya's critical viewpoint.

"He's a good friend."

"I think he'd like to be more. If that's the case, you'd be a fool not to accept. Stephen Camden is quite a catch."

If only it were that simple. Just a matter of securing her future with no thought of how her action would affect their lives. Maybe she should stop being so conscience-stricken and go with her heart. No. Loving Stephen made her want his happiness more than she wanted her own.

Genny glanced toward the bassinet. Jonathan slept on, oblivious to the adult chatter.

"And as usual you're not sure," Sonya said with a shake of her head. "Don't you ever jump in and enjoy life?"

"I've prayed about it."

Sonya snorted. "Since when do you pray?"

When had she slipped back into the habit? It had been a gradual thing since coming to live near Stephen. She prayed for his safety, her child's healing, Sonya, and for her own guidance. She had conversations with God on a number of lonely nights, and He'd answered her prayers.

Genny felt out of sorts. Being around Sonya often made her feel that way. "Maybe if you'd sought God's counsel on your investment, you would still have the money."

"You know I don't believe in that stuff."

"It's not stuff, Sonya. You came in search of support, but you never had to leave home. Jesus wants to be your friend in times of trouble." Stephen had shared these truths with her when she felt confused.

"Yeah, sure."

"Psalm 46:1 says that God is our refuge and strength. If you show a little faith, He'll work miracles in your life."

"I'm going to take a shower."

For years, Genny had invited Sonya to church and tried to talk to her about God's love, and for all those years Sonya's response had been to ignore her.

"We'll have to share the bed. I'll take the side near the bassinet since Jonathan will probably wake during the night."

"I need my sleep."

Her attitude bothered Genny. She didn't want to share her bed with Sonya either. "You can have half the bed, the sofa, or the floor. Take your pick."

"The sofa."

"I'll get you a blanket," Genny said. I will not let you get under my skin, she vowed when Sonya disappeared into the bathroom.

❧

Sonya slept on the following morning as Genny dressed herself and Jonathan for the day. Unsure about Stephen's plans, Genny decided to play it by ear. After feeding Jonathan, she made the bed and started work.

Stretching luxuriously when she woke, Sonya threw her legs off the sofa. "What are you doing?"

"Working."

"I'm calling in sick," Sonya said, grinning slyly when Genny's eyebrows shot up in surprise. "I'm entitled."

"I want to hear more about this deal. I think you should have some legal recourse," Genny said.

"I need a bath."

Sonya spent over an hour in the bathroom and came out wearing the clothes from the previous evening.

"Why don't we go shopping this afternoon?" Sonya suggested over lunch. "You're earning money now," she coaxed at Genny's refusal. "Why not buy some new clothes?"

Genny didn't explain the reasons behind her need to save every dime. "I can't afford to throw money away."

"From the state of your wardrobe, I'd hardly call it a wasteful investment."

Unfortunately Sonya spoke the truth. Pregnancy had rearranged her body and her clothes fit differently now. "Maybe one outfit," Genny relented.

"For Stephen," Sonya said with a pleased smile. "A woman wants to look good for the man in her life. Just think how you could splurge if you were married. Imagine the gown you would have worn to the awards ceremony."

Her imagination barely stretched to the depth of her feelings for Stephen. Considering all the ways being the woman in his life would change hers frightened Genny.

"We can go after I drop these letters off at the office and pick up the mailbags."

Stephen insisted on keeping Jonathan for her. He promised to call his lawyer.

Still trying to catch her breath two hours later, Genny sorted through the racks in yet another store. She had no idea how many places they had visited nor how many pieces of clothing she had tried on at Sonya's insistence.

"You did remarkably well in losing the extra pounds," Sonya commented as Genny modeled the skintight dress.

Genny didn't care for the garment at all. "There's never been much shape to me."

Sonya sighed impatiently. "Take it off. It's not you either. Definitely the jeans. But you need a smaller size."

By the time they finished, Sonya had talked her into a new dress, a silk blouse, a pair of soft leather boots that were on sale, and the jeans. Satisfaction with her new clothes won out over practicality. Genny tucked her bags in the trunk and went around to the passenger seat.

"You can wear them when Stephen takes you out."

They had never been on a real date. "I don't like leaving Jonathan."

"Don't be silly," Sonya snapped with familiar impatience. "It won't hurt to leave him with a sitter."

Genny looked out the car window. "That's what Stephen says." They couldn't understand her reluctance to be center stage. "I'm not comfortable in crowds."

"I don't think Stephen's ashamed of you."

"Sometimes I wish I were a sexy, younger woman."

Sonya's eyes drifted from the road. "Maybe you should let him decide what he needs. If it's you, all the better."

When they drove into the yard, Stephen carried the bundled baby out to greet them. "Hello, ladies," he called, focusing on Genny. "Miss me?"

No way would she admit how much. "Sonya kept me busy."

Stephen followed her around the car. "I hope you bought something special for tonight."

"What are you planning?"

"I want to get everyone together for dinner."

"Where?" she asked, swallowing the butterflies that stirred in her stomach.

"My place." Stephen followed them into the guesthouse.

Sonya disappeared into the bathroom with her purchases.

Genny flung her purse and bags on the bed. She took Jonathan from Stephen and carried him into the nursery. As she leaned over the side of the crib and whispered to the baby, Stephen's arms slipped about her waist.

"How are things between you and Sonya?" he asked softly.

Jonathan's eyes drifted closed, and she took Stephen's hand and led him from the room. "Sonya doesn't seem as upset. She offered to help finish the fan mail this morning, but never got around to it. Oh, I forgot the mailbags."

"I'll get them later."

They walked into the kitchen. "Chuck Harper introduced himself while we were at the office."

"What did he say?"

Genny thought he sounded suspicious. "Nothing much. He and Sonya seemed to hit it off right away. He said to tell you hello and that he'll be glad when the two weeks are up."

"Good old Chuck. Always hammering home his point."

Genny eyed him curiously. "Stephen, is it good for you to take time right now?"

He didn't look her in the eye. "We all need a vacation."

"Yes, but is it the best time for everyone? I mean. . . Well, I know you wanted to be here when Jonathan came home but what about the others?"

"No one's complaining, Gen. The guys are glad I put my foot down. I gave Harper sufficient warning, and the timing's perfect. Let me tell you what I have in mind for tonight. I thought we'd order a pizza and watch a movie. I have several I've never seen."

They were the kind of plans Genny could appreciate. "What about Sonya? Is she invited?"

"Three guests—you, Jonathan, and Sonya."

"Sounds wonderful." She hung her coat in the closet. "Did you talk with the attorney yet?"

"He's checking, but when I shared what you told me, he thought Sonya knew she was taking a big risk. He'd read about the stock and said it sounded iffy."

Genny frowned. "But surely she wouldn't gamble away that much money?"

"If she was eager to advance herself, she may have considered it a worthwhile risk."

"Oh, I hope not."

❧

It was a cozy evening. Stephen ordered the pizza and had the DVD queued up by the time they arrived at the house.

As soon as the movie started, Jonathan turned fretful. Genny attempted to pass him to Sonya so she could warm his bottle.

"He'll wrinkle my skirt," she demurred.

"I'll take him." Stephen made Jonathan comfortable.

Genny stopped just outside the doorway and glanced back. Stephen's behavior was so different from that first time. Jonathan's presence made no difference to him. He had become very comfortable with her son.

&

Sonya's day off stretched into three before she decided to go home. If her condo hadn't been big enough for them, the guesthouse had to feel less than cozy to Sonya.

Her determination to interfere with Genny's work came out in all sorts of petty ways. It was like having a second child demanding her time. Sonya repeatedly insisted they go shopping, and having fulfilled her wardrobe needs to the extent of her budget on their first outing, Genny refused. Sonya pouted.

Sonya continued to ignore Jonathan.

Genny insisted they not disturb Stephen, but he checked in frequently. When he detected Sonya's presence was affecting Genny, he suggested they do things together.

Slay and Ronnie baby-sat a second night for Stephen to take Genny and Sonya to an expensive restaurant.

Her sister seemed to have forgotten her feud with Stephen. Their parents had been socialites and evidently Sonya inherited every bit of their people skills. While Genny could be happy at a fast-food restaurant, Sonya was right in her element with the costly surroundings and unpriced menu.

They placed their drink orders, Genny and Stephen opting for iced tea. Sonya chose a mixed drink. After a third, she became almost giddy.

"I'm off to the little girl's room."

They watched her stagger away. "I'm sorry," Genny whispered.

He squeezed her hand. "You're not responsible for her behavior."

"I know, but you're doing this for me."

"Exactly. I'll tolerate Sonya for the opportunity to be with you." He laid his hand over hers. "How much longer does she plan to stay?"

"I felt certain she'd have gone back to work by now. I pray it's soon," Genny admitted.

"Look who I found," Sonya cried, dragging Chuck Harper toward their table. "I insisted he join us for a drink."

"You've had enough, Sonya," Genny warned.

Sonya giggled and said, "Would you believe she's the little sister?" Her behavior became even more excitable, her laughter almost raucous. "On second thought, I think she must be adopted. She doesn't act like anyone in our family."

Noting Genny's distress, Stephen motioned to the waiter. "Bring the lady a coffee, please."

"The lady wants another of these," Sonya said, waving the glass. When the liquid splashed at the waiter's feet, Sonya broke into hysterical laughter.

"The phones are ringing off the hook," Chuck said, taking the focus off Sonya.

"Let 'em ring," Stephen said.

The manager appeared none too happy. "So how's the time off going? You feeling relaxed?"

"Getting there."

Sonya wrapped her arm about Chuck's, sitting indecently close to him. "Let's don't talk business," she said, the telltale signs of too much drink showing in her voice. "How long have you and Stephen been friends?"

Genny noted Stephen's grimace.

"We've worked together for what," he glanced at Stephen, "five or six years?"

"Five." Stephen took a bite of his salmon.

Sonya flashed Chuck a brilliant smile. "I'm so glad I ran into you."

"You're certainly a bright spot in my day."

The waiter returned and set the coffee on the table. "Your party has arrived, Mr. Harper."

"Put this bill on my tab," he instructed the waiter as he pushed his chair from the table.

"Forget it, Harper. I'm treating these two lovely ladies."

"Oh, come on, Steve, you're my star performer."

"Yeah, Steve, he's just trying to be nice," Sonya defended.

Genny found Sonya's breathy words and behavior nauseating. Stephen was obviously uncomfortable, and Genny wished they'd stayed home.

"Fine," Stephen agreed reluctantly. "Thanks for the meal."

"Yes, thanks, Chuckie."

Chuck Harper grinned. "Good seeing you again, Mrs. Smith. I'll be in touch, Stephen. Sonya, drop by the office sometime. I'm always interested in another professional's ideas."

"Would you like to leave?" Genny asked Stephen.

"No," Sonya wailed. "I'm enjoying myself."

"Too much," he muttered. "You should know he's a married man."

"It's not like we're having an affair," Sonya said loudly.

Genny hazarded a guess that Sonya might jump at the opportunity if it were offered.

"Just as well," Stephen said. "You need to be careful where Chuck's concerned."

The nightmarish evening ended, and Genny insisted they go to the guesthouse when Sonya wanted to linger after Slay and Ronnie left.

"I'll talk to you tomorrow," Stephen called when she followed Sonya out the door. "I thought we might visit a nursery or two."

"Sounds good. Sleep tight and God bless."

He winked at her. "You too."

At the guesthouse, Sonya disappeared into the bathroom. She came out complaining of a headache, and Genny fought back the desire to share a few home truths with her. She took her turn in the bathroom instead. Jonathan's cries caught her attention, and Genny found Sonya fast asleep on the sofa.

Sonya disappeared for a couple of hours the following morning and came over to Stephen's when she returned.

"Genny, I'm heading home. Just need to pick up my things before I hit the road."

"I'll help." Hopefully she didn't sound too eager.

"Jonathan can stay with me if you girls want a few minutes alone."

In the guesthouse, Genny helped Sonya gather the items she'd slung over the small space.

"So what have you two been doing this morning?"

Genny looked at her. "Talking. Playing with Jonathan."

Sonya appeared to find the idea distasteful. "Is that all you ever do?"

"Stephen and I are friends."

"You're blind as a bat if you can't see that man's in love with you."

Sonya's interest in their relationship disturbed Genny. "So what are your plans?"

"Back to the office for now. Guess I'll have to concentrate on finding myself a wealthy man."

As Stephen suggested, they learned Sonya had known the chance she was taking. The money was gone, gambled on a less than sure bet.

Once Sonya left, they spent a lot of time together. When she said she had to work, Stephen would help with the mail. They lounged around home, watched movies, prepared meals together, planned the landscaping in further detail, and went to church.

Two weeks passed quickly and when the bus pulled away, Genny felt as if a part of her was on board.

sixteen

Genny decided the best way to stop missing Stephen was to jump back into her routine as quickly as possible. She stopped by the office to drop off the mail and pick up the newest batch. Tracie, the receptionist, insisted on holding Jonathan while the bags were being unloaded and loaded.

"If the mail keeps up like that, they'll have to start delivering it to the house for you."

Genny nodded. "We really need to go."

"Don't be in such a rush," Tracie insisted. "The fans aren't that impatient. Besides, I need your help. We're planning something for Stephen's birthday. Any ideas?"

The casual question floored Genny. Even though they had discussed age, she didn't know his actual birth date. "When?"

"One month from today. He's turning thirty."

How was she supposed to make suggestions for his party when she hardly knew him? She knew so little about Stephen. Certainly not the date of his birth, the names of his parents or grandparents. None of the things she'd known about John before they married. The same went for Stephen. He knew nothing of her past. He might not want a life with her once he knew the truth.

Genny reached for the baby. "Can I get back to you?"

"Sure. We've got time. Bye-bye, Sweetie." Tracie waved to the baby.

She didn't have a clue as to how to organize a big birthday celebration. There had been no major birthday productions, generally dinner at home or in a restaurant with guests limited to Sonya or some of John's contractor buddies. A time or two the neighbors had been invited over for a barbecue.

Always the gifts were practical, new clothes or tools. She

wanted to give Stephen something special. The lack of an idea troubled her.

He could buy anything he wanted. Actually there wasn't much he didn't already own. She selected and discarded ideas. The landscaping was out of the question. Her budget wouldn't allow for the purchase of shrubs and trees.

She put Jonathan to bed and straightened the sitting area. As she folded a knitted afghan over the sofa arm, an idea planted itself. What about a sweater? Stephen admired her work. She had time, and it would be an original, made with love.

As her enthusiasm grew, Genny spent hours looking for the perfect yarn for the pattern she selected. The specialty shop was her last hope.

"That's it!" Genny cried when the sales assistant showed her a silvery gray. "That's exactly what I want."

Genny paid the clerk and hurried to the grocery store next door. As always, she felt excited about the new project.

She picked up the items she needed and wheeled her cart into the checkout line and passed the time scanning tabloid headlines. They seemed more sensational than usual. *A thirty-pound baby? Who writes this stuff?* She read on, her gaze jerking back to a tiny photo in the lower left corner. It couldn't be.

"Come on, Lady, I don't have all day," the man behind her barked.

"Sorry." Genny grabbed the paper and shoved her cart forward. After the clerk scanned the price, she folded and stuffed it into her purse.

A few people were staring at her. Genny swiped her debit card, grabbed Jonathan's carrier, and hurried out the door. Her steps quickened when she heard someone behind her.

"Lady, you forgot your bag." The young man held the groceries she'd just purchased.

"Sorry. I mean, thanks."

At the car, Genny set the bag in the car and secured Jonathan's seat. Jerking the paper open, her fingers shook as

she fumbled through the pages in search of the article. He
blood ran cold at the pictures of her with Stephen. And then
the photos of her parents. She should have told him.

Somehow she managed to get herself, Jonathan, and the ca
home in one piece.

The answering machine light flashed in rapid succession
indicating a number of messages. Dread filled her as she hi
the play button, and Stephen's voice floated into the room.

She jotted down the number, cringing at the coolness in his
tone when he said he'd called for security.

Her feet dragged as she put the groceries away. First, she
needed to read the article. Then she could talk to Stephen.

Dropping onto the sofa, Genny read the article. Just as
she'd feared—her family history was the main thrust of the
tabloid nightmare. Stephen was mentioned often, the facts
skewed deceptively.

The phone rang. Genny reached for the cordless.

"Where have you been?"

Stephen. She closed her eyes and drew in a deep breath. "I
stopped by the office to pick up the mail and did a little
shopping."

"You've seen the rag, haven't you?"

Her heart raced. "Just now."

"Why, Genny? You had to know it would come out sooner
or later."

"It never came up." The moment the words were out she
wished them back.

"And you owe me nothing." Stephen's tone veered quickly
to anger.

"I owe you everything," she countered. "I warned you there
were things in my past. I didn't want you hurt."

His tone softened. "Don't worry about me. I need to know
one thing. Did you release the information?"

Genny was horrified. "I would never do that. How could
you even think it?"

"I don't." His agitation carried over the long distance. "You remember that day at the hospital? The reporters? I thought Chuck set them on us. He assures me he didn't, but if it wasn't him, then who?"

"It was public record nineteen years ago," Genny said. "Anyone could have dug it up. Maybe as background research on the woman in your life. I'm sorry, Stephen."

"I hope it's not too late to mitigate the damage," he said. "I'll see if the attorney thinks we should tell the story to a reputable magazine or just let it die a natural death."

"This isn't going to hurt you in any way, is it?"

"I was thinking of you and Jonathan. I don't want reporters hounding either of you. It's important that he lead a normal life."

Genny noted Stephen's controlled anger. No doubt his lips were compressed with the emotion. "Stephen, I'm really sorry."

"Don't be. Obviously, I haven't worked hard enough at earning your trust. I wish you'd realize your past isn't a good enough reason to give up on our future, but somehow you think it is."

"Trust had nothing to do with it, Stephen. I didn't tell you because I wanted to forget it ever happened."

"Trust has everything to do with it, Genny. You didn't trust me enough to tell the truth about your parents. You don't trust me enough to marry me. You don't trust me to take care of you and Jonathan."

"Stephen, it's not that—"

"Genny, it's obvious. It doesn't matter how I feel about you if I can't get past your doubts. Just let security deal with the press, because whether you believe it or not, we only have your best interests at heart."

A dial tone replaced his voice.

What had she done? "Oh, God, why did I have to hurt him so?" she sobbed in despair.

Why should she trust God? What had He done to make her life easier? Her parents hated each other. They'd destroyed

each other. He'd sent John. They were having marital problems. He'd given them a child. Jonathan was premature and
could have died. He'd sent Stephen. Sonya didn't want them
in her home. He'd sent Stephen.

Could Stephen be the answer to an unspoken prayer?
Hadn't God looked out for her even when she hadn't trusted
Him fully?

Genny found herself running on adrenaline over the next
hours. When security recommended that she stay at Stephen's
house, she agreed. She tried to occupy her time with the
correspondence.

Stephen's words kept coming back to her. Did she want to
spend the rest of her life trusting no one but herself?

The yarn lay on the desktop, tempting her to start work.
She went into his closet and checked another sweater. Once
there, she lingered, absorbing the scents she associated with
Stephen. She missed him terribly.

"Mrs. Smith?"

"In here." She moved to the doorway.

"There's a Ronnie Slayman here to see you."

"Let her in."

Genny smiled at the woman's playful grimace when she followed the guard into the living room. "I feel like I've stumbled into Fort Knox," the willowy blond teased. "I've never
seen so much security."

"Stephen's doing. For some reason he thinks more is better."

Ronnie grinned. "Isn't it?"

A smile crept over Genny's face. "Sometimes."

"Are you okay?"

"I've been better. What about you? How are mother and
child?"

Ronnie rubbed a hand over her extended stomach. "Mother
is getting impatient. Nine months never seemed so long."

Genny smiled. "Don't rush things. You'll be holding your
baby before you know it."

"I can't say I won't mind not being pregnant," Ronnie

admitted. "And it'll be wonderful to have this little part of Slay to keep me company when he's on the road. Coming home to loved ones is important to the guys. Their touring schedule is not what it's cracked up to be."

"I know Stephen gets very tired of traveling. Still, it would be a shame for them not to perform. They are so talented."

Ronnie studied Genny openly. "Slay says he's never seen Steve so happy."

Genny's eyes closed and she took a deep breath. "I can't tell you how that frightens me."

"Why?"

"Look at me, Ronnie. Do I look like Stephen's type?"

"Obviously Steve likes what he sees," Ronnie said. "Slay told me what happened. Stephen fired Harper on the spot. And not a moment too soon if you ask me. That man is a tyrant."

Following the woman's rapid-fire conversation took some doing on Genny's part. "Their manager? What did he have to do with this?"

"Steve warned him to leave you alone. When he learned Harper was involved in producing that trash, that was the end."

Genny blanched at Ronnie's words. The story of her life "trash"? Come to think of it, that seemed a fairly apt description. "But Stephen said Chuck Harper didn't have anything to do with the publicity."

"Well, he did."

Genny wandered to the window. Outside there was more activity than she would have considered her life warranted. She turned back to Ronnie. "How do you stand this fishbowl?"

"I don't. The guys do. I know Slay had a tough time getting used to the loss of privacy. They accept the fans and publicity, but that doesn't mean they wouldn't love to shut the door on that aspect of their lives. After the incident with Bobby, I thought the phones would never stop ringing."

"Bobby?"

Sadness touched Ronnie's face. "He was a member of the

band. Bobby was a troubled kid. He overdosed on drugs. I think they all felt responsible. Stephen said they should have done more."

The revelation hit Genny like a 120-volt charge. Stephen hadn't been totally honest with her either. "What could they have done?"

"Exactly what they did. The kid was old enough to make his own decisions. Unfortunately, guilt and hindsight are powerful motivators. They need to understand it wasn't their fault. Learn to trust their instincts again."

And she had to learn to trust the man she loved too much to give up. "Ronnie, I need to ask a really big favor. Can you take care of Jonathan for a couple of days? I need to see Stephen."

seventeen

Genny glanced out the plane window, wondering how Stephen would react to her arrival. This time she would do the surprising. It didn't matter that this little escapade nearly wiped out her savings. She was a woman with a purpose.

She almost surprised herself with the efficiency with which she handled this trip. Her faith that Ronnie would take good care of Jonathan helped. Leaving the plane with her carry-on, Genny caught a cab to the hotel.

Ray answered the phone when she called up to the room. "Steve just went out. He'll be furious he missed you."

They hadn't talked since Stephen accused her of not trusting him. "He won't miss me. I'm calling from the lobby."

"I'll be right down."

A broad grin covered Ray's face as he walked down the hallway from the elevator. "Stephen's doing a sound check. He's planning to leave for home right after the show. Where's Jonathan?"

"With Ronnie and that security army Stephen hired. So can you get a girl good seats at tonight's concert?"

"Not a concert. A gig at our favorite club. There's a table front row center. Right where Stephen can keep an eye on you."

Genny grinned. "Perfect. I need to change."

A twinkle surfaced deep in the man's eyes. "Something tells me Steve's life is never going to be the same again."

"No different than it's been since the first night we crossed paths."

Ray picked up her bag and led the way to the elevators. The doors closed, and Ray took advantage of the privacy. "Steve came very close to walking out, but after the mess with Harper he had to stay."

"I don't understand about Chuck Harper. What does he have to do with this?"

"The article was another of his publicity stunts. Steve fired him on the spot. Had security take him out."

"That's what Ronnie said. But Stephen said he told him he wasn't responsible. Who supplied the information?"

Ray clammed up, his bottomless well of information appearing to have run dry. Genny was immediately suspicious. What was he not telling her? "Let's catch up with Steve. He'll fill you in on the specifics."

"Do you think he'll forgive me for not telling him?"

"Stephen doesn't blame you, Genny. He knows you were just a child."

He gave her more credit than she deserved. "Not a child, Ray. I was seventeen. I married John a few months later. I thought if I pretended long enough it would go away. It hasn't."

"I can't say I blame you. I told Steve to take care in judging since he had no idea what you'd lived through." Ray unlocked the door and moved back to allow her inside. "That's Steve's room. You can change in there. Steve and I have the suite this time. We take turns so everybody gets a chance to feel invaded. It's where we gather to wind down after a show."

That explained the party in his room. "Will he come back to change?"

"He took his things with him. He has a 1:00 A.M. flight."

"When do we need to leave?"

"Twenty minutes ago. It's a miracle I came back."

As the cab pulled into the parking area of the club, Genny fought the feeling she didn't belong here. Part of her discomfort had to do with the location. In the past, a concert, a nice restaurant, or a dinner theater had been the extent of her entertainment search.

"What's wrong?"

She shrugged. "I'm scared."

"Don't be. Jerry's helped a lot of groups get their start. We try to get here at least once a year. Ready? It's almost time for us to go on."

Stephen was not in sight when Ray seated Genny at the large table before the stage.

"What would you like to drink?"

She told Ray, and he gestured for a waitress and gave the order. "Say a prayer for me," she whispered.

"I can't wait to see Steve's face when he catches sight of you." Ray winked and moved toward the stage.

The lights came up and with the first sounds of music, couples moved to the dance floor.

Genny's gaze zeroed in on Stephen. Their gazes locked.

She broke eye contact first, taking a sip of her soft drink when her throat became dry. As if drawn, Genny looked at him again. She stared deep into Stephen's eyes, smiled at his audacious wink, and toyed with her glass when she grew shy. Each time she looked up, Stephen turned up the wattage, the smoky gray eyes burning with love. Genny smiled, this time not looking away.

The mood changed, the lights dimming. Stephen pulled the microphone toward him. "This song is dedicated to my special lady."

He let go and swung his guitar around to strum the first chords of the romantic ballad. Genny blushed furiously when curious eyes turned her way. She had to get used to this—for Stephen.

All too soon it was over, and he said, "And now let's liven things up a little."

A group of dancers two-stepped around the floor.

"Let's dance."

The voice sounded in her ear, and Genny smelled the liquor on his breath before she looked up at the strange man. "No, thank you," she murmured, turning her attention back to the stage.

"Just one dance," he repeated, wobbling slightly as the alcohol slurred his persistent plea.

Genny sought Stephen's help. As if by magic a huge, burly man appeared at her table.

"This guy bothering you?"

"I'm sure he doesn't mean to," Genny allowed graciously.

"You heard the lady. Take a walk."

The man wandered off, and Genny turned to her rescuer with a heartfelt, "Thank you."

"My pleasure. Name's Jerry Todd."

"You're Stephen's friend," Genny exclaimed. "Ray told me about you."

"Then I'm surprised you're speaking to me." Jerry laughed at his joke. His laughter was as big as he was. "What's your poison?"

"Soda."

"Another teetotaler. I should have known. Let me order you a drink. No alcohol, I promise," he assured when she refused. Jerry caught a passing waitress and ordered.

The drink had the appearance of a glass of fruit juice. Genny took a sip and found the fruity flavor delicious. "It's not your usual," she admitted.

Jerry smiled. "It started as a joke. Cowboy Jamboree performed here the day their first song hit the charts. The bartender felt it reason to celebrate and improved Steve's usual orange juice. The C. J. Special caught on from there. Steve still does his without alcohol."

"Please have a seat, Mr. Todd," she invited. "I'm Genny."

"Jerry. Some crowd, huh? They can pack 'em in tighter than sardines. I'd have to build a bigger place if they were regulars."

"From what Ray said, they owe you a great deal."

"Steve and I pulled our stretch together in the military. When we came home, I invested my money in The Rodeo. At first Steve was my star act. Then the band formed, and they played here a lot too. He's paid me back many times with the good publicity he gives the club."

"I didn't know he was in the military," she said, glancing up as Stephen sang the last chorus and stepped back for Ray to sing the next number. His hair and forehead were damp with perspiration.

"How come we haven't seen you around here before?"

"Thanks to Stephen, I have an infant son who keeps me home."

His brows lifted. Genny realized her blunder and hurriedly explained Stephen's role in her son's birth.

Jerry's eyes crinkled merrily. "For a moment there, I thought my old buddy had been keeping secrets. What's his name?"

"Jonathan Andrew." Genny reached for the photograph she kept handy.

Jerry nodded appreciatively. "He's a fine boy."

"Thanks. I'm glad we got to meet. If you're ever in Memphis, you'll have to come for dinner one night when Stephen's home."

"It's a date. Just let me know when."

"Date?" Stephen repeated as he walked up behind her. "Trying to steal my girl, Jerry?"

"This one's only got eyes for you."

Stephen grinned and took the chair beside Genny's. "And I plan to keep it that way. Thanks for stepping in. I was about to come off that stage."

"I noticed. He won't bother her again. Jim likes a pretty face only as long as it likes him in return."

"I owe you one." Stephen's arm snaked about the back of her chair.

"Genny showed me a photo of her boy."

"Handsome little guy, don't you think?" Stephen bragged. "He's come a long way in such a short time, hasn't he, Sweetheart?"

Stunned by the pride in his voice, she nodded.

"Steve's one. . .uh, sweet guy himself, Genny," Jerry said, "but I suppose you know that already."

"More so every day."

A strange, faintly eager look flashed into Stephen's eyes.

"Enough of this mutual admiration stuff. How about explaining why you're here."

"I think that's my cue to exit."

"Thanks for the rescue," she called as Jerry moved across the room.

"Any time."

"Genny, where are the security people?" Stephen demanded.

"Probably filing a missing person's report. I'm AWOL."

❧

Stephen ignored her droll comment. A knowing smile blossomed to fullness. "Having a good time?" he whispered against her ear.

"Wonderful."

"You shouldn't flirt with me like that. I hope the audience didn't notice when I stumbled over the words."

Genny studied the crowd.

"I see what you mean about these places," Genny said when a couple danced past, their bodies glued to each other. "Not exactly your church social."

Stephen's sigh warmed her ear. "Compared to some places we've performed, this place is tame. Just one more reason why I want out."

"I've been thinking about that."

"Oh no," Stephen groaned, his playful grimace bringing laughter.

"No, really, this is serious. You aren't the same struggling band you were all those years ago when you played in honky-tonks. People love and admire you, and if you let your light shine during interviews and record the hymns when you can, they'll know. And where is it written that you can't record a solo album if you want?"

"Nowhere that I know of," Stephen said, appearing to give the matter consideration. "So you're saying not to hide my light under a bushel, stay where I am, and be a witness the Lord would be proud of?"

Genny nodded. "I know you're not exactly happy, but what

if it's where the Lord wants you?"

"I'd never thought of it that way."

"I'm praying for you too."

Stephen covered her hand with his, smiling broadly. "It's so wonderful to hear you say that. Have you made your peace with the Lord?"

"We've worked things out. You'd better go. They're motioning you onstage."

"Okay, but we have unfinished business. Oh, and don't you think maybe you should call the house and let them know where you are?"

"Ronnie will tell them."

The concert ended late. Genny and Steve rode to the hotel in a cab. She had no idea where the others went when she and Stephen returned to the suite.

"Hello, Darling," he whispered. "I missed you."

Her arms went about his neck. "I had to come. Oh, Stephen, I'm so sorry."

"Why? What was so important it couldn't wait?"

"This," she whispered, kissing him again. "I had to tell you I love you. I couldn't bear you thinking I don't trust you."

"Oh, Gen. The situation caught me unaware. I should have known you'd tell me when the time was right. I felt disappointed because I wanted you to confide in me."

"I'm sorry about the way I've behaved, but I need to know why you want to marry me."

Stephen pulled away, grasping her hand in his and leading the way to the sofa. "I know you had the perfect relationship with your first husband and maybe we'll never come close. . ."

"We've surpassed anything John and I ever had," Genny admitted softly. "That's the most frightening aspect, knowing you're as close to perfect as anyone can get. I'm afraid I can't measure up."

"To what? I love you, Baby. That night we met, there was something so right about my being there. In the space of a few hours, I found I never wanted to leave you or Jonathan again." Genny gasped at his words. "You invaded my thoughts, filled my heart and mind. I crave your kindness and gentleness for myself. I'm not perfect, Genny. I never promise to be, but I do love you."

Tears slid down her cheeks. "That's not true. You're too perfect for me. You were so right about my not trusting in God. I kept seeing the things that happened in my life as His doing. I finally realized something good came out of every bad thing that happened."

"Then why won't you say yes to my proposal?"

"Because we don't know each other well enough yet." Genny swallowed the knot in her throat. "I'm sorry I didn't tell you the truth, but I'm ready to accept your love."

"Oh, Genny."

He moved to hug her, and she pushed him away with forceful determination. "Wait, I have to tell you about my parents. It's not a story I'm proud of. It's not even something I understand. John shielded me from the pain. I'm not going to let you do the same."

"I love you, Genny."

"I'll never be the woman you deserve."

"But you'll be the woman God intends for me. Perfection is the pinnacle we all strive for but rarely achieve. I want you to love me, with all my faults. I'm human with all the human failings you can name, but God forgives me when I sin, and I move forward in my efforts to be the man He would have me be. The only perfection I want to achieve is in going to heaven when I die and making our marriage last for at least fifty years or so."

"Oh, Stephen, I do love you. Almost too much if that's possible. My insecurities make me see the things you do as attempts to control my life. When Ronnie told me how you'd kicked yourself over Bobby's death, I understood why you had to help."

"It's important to be there for the people you love."

Genny tried to look at him but ended up looking at her hands, the emerald ring she'd placed on her finger that night. "Everything happened so quickly. I met you and my feelings escalated out of control. That made me more insecure. Maybe it's misplaced loyalty. I felt unfaithful to the memory of my son's father. I need to keep him alive for Jonathan. I thought I couldn't do that if I loved you. And I want to be more confident, at least a little pretty, for you."

"Sweetie, I like what I see. But even more, I like what I feel with I'm with you." He held her close for several minutes.

Genny lifted her head from his chest. "Who told the press my father killed my mother? Ray's fount of information dried up like a creek bed in a drought when I asked."

He seemed reluctant. "Sonya. Harper may have provided the gun, but she pulled the trigger. She went after the fast buck."

Genny twisted the ring about her finger. "She's like them. Everything in her world revolves around money and prestige. My parents would be alive today if they'd cared about anyone besides themselves."

Could I have changed things? She asked herself the same question every time she thought about that afternoon. "It was a couple of weeks before my high school graduation. I came home early and found my parents arguing. Their fights were always so violent. Almost deadly. There was no place to run."

"Was it different from before?"

She nodded. "They didn't know I was home." Stephen hugged her closer. "Mother screamed that she'd stayed long enough. She wanted the divorce Daddy had promised her all those years ago.

"Mother was cruel. She just kept hacking away at his pride, saying awful, hurtful things. She told him he was a lousy husband. Daddy slapped her. Her scream was the last thing I heard before I ran away. The police were there when I came home. Mother was dead. She'd hit her head on the stairs and broken her neck.

"The press had a field day. Mother was running for judge,

and Daddy was a prominent doctor. Sonya was so unforgiving. She pitied Daddy's stupidity. Said he should have given Mother her divorce. She doubted they had ever loved each other."

Stephen dropped a kiss on her brow. "Was it always bad?"

"Just around Sonya and me. They were social creatures. Publicly, they tolerated each other. I'm sure people were convinced they loved one another."

"Honey, I'm sorry. I didn't realize how traumatic this was for you."

"That's not all," she continued. "It was ruled accidental, but Daddy couldn't handle what he'd done. His staff found him dead. They said it was a heart attack, but he had no medical history. The autopsy revealed he had injected himself with insulin. He tried to provide for us by leaving a large life insurance policy. It didn't pay because of the suicide.

"Sonya was angrier about the money than she was with Daddy for taking his own life. She missed our lavish lifestyle. She dropped out of college and took a job, claiming she needed to be there for me. I think she was too embarrassed to stay in school. I should have told you this before. Maybe if we'd taken time to know each other, I would have."

"I know everything I need to know about you. You're a special person. Don't you know that?"

"I've always needed someone to tell me. Until you, John was the only person who ever said he loved me."

"I don't expect you to be dependent on me."

"I can't be. I loved being a homemaker, but now I have a child. I need to be able to provide for him."

As the words left her lips, the truth struck Genny. She constantly spouted off about providing for Jonathan, but Stephen had provided the means. He'd provided her independence and she'd been too blind to see it. She misinterpreted his caring actions as charity when they were so much more.

"You want to be the perfect mother," Stephen said. "You think it's your fault that Jonathan was premature. Personally,

I think it's remarkable you did as well as you did."

"Maybe you know me better than I know myself. I always tried to make up for my shortcomings by being the best wife I could be. When that was gone, I was pregnant and scared and forced to live a life I hated. Now I have to do things for myself, and you have to love me enough to let me."

"Honey, the only condition on my love is that you love me as much as I love you."

Genny found it too easy to get lost in the way he looked at her. "I'm too old for you."

"More experienced," Stephen whispered.

"Too insecure."

"Oh, really?" he asked more boldly. "Well, Genevieve Smith, you can be very secure about my love."

Silence filled the room as he kissed her thoroughly. Genny wrapped her arms about his neck and murmured, "I'm afraid I won't be woman enough to make you happy forever."

In his eyes, Genny saw the passion of loving. "If you can't, no one else ever will."

eighteen

"Are you sure you want to do this?" Stephen asked.

"I have to confront Sonya. This vendetta has to stop."

"You want me to go with you?"

Genny slipped on her coat and smoothed her gloves into place. "I can handle this myself."

"Will you tell her we're getting married?"

"When I have to." At his pained expression, she said, "I don't plan to give her any news to impart to the press."

He nodded understanding. "Will you come to the house when you get back?"

"The moment I return."

Throughout the long drive, Genny struggled to come up with the right questions for Sonya. Only one that required an answer. Why?

The truth about what had happened with their parents was always in Genny's thoughts. If she had told them to stop, the ending might have been different.

She timed her arrival for when she could be certain Sonya was home. A light shone in the upstairs bedroom. Genny parked and went to the front door, listening to Sonya's loud muttering about late visitors as she came down the stairs.

"Well, well, to what do I owe the honor?" Sonya asked, grinning as she leaned against the doorjamb. "As if I don't already know. I don't suppose you ever got around to telling Stephen about your secret life."

Sonya couldn't know how hate-filled their mother's words had been, and yet the same mean-spirited behavior colored her words.

"It was an accident," Genny maintained in steadfast defense of her father.

"Bury your head in the sand. At least Stephen knows the truth now."

"Why?"

"They offered me good money for news on the lady Stephen's so desperate to protect. I think Chuck Harper was even more impressed after the 'scandal' came out." The way she used her fingers as quotation marks made Genny flinch. "He probably figured Stephen would dump you fast when he heard the news. It didn't happen though, did it?"

"Stephen understands."

"And Lucky Genny comes out on top again."

Sonya's voice carried in the clear evening air. Genny glanced around, uncomfortable airing their dirty laundry in public.

"Oh, for heaven's sake, come in," Sonya snapped, leaving the door wide open as she swept into the living room.

Genny followed, shutting the door behind her. Sonya had redecorated with new furniture, an Oriental rug, and expensive artwork. Were the ill-gotten gains the source of her decorating budget?

"What do you think?" she asked, whirling about happily. "I love it. I'm not ashamed to invite people over now."

There was nothing wrong with the old stuff. It couldn't have been more than a few months old. "I can't believe the levels you stoop to for a dollar."

"Oh, if you only knew."

Sonya's evil sneer disturbed Genny. "What have you done?"

"You really don't have a clue?"

"Sonya, so help me if you do one more thing to hurt Stephen or his career, I'll—"

"Pray for me?" Sonya laughed. "Grow up, Gen. You're as naïve as the day you were born. It's time you woke up. You never knew we were about to pull the plug on your safe, secure world. Didn't you ever wonder why there was no insurance? Why everything was in hock?"

"John was too young for insurance."

"John was an old man when you married him," Sonya said

with heavy irony. "We were going away together when you messed things up with your news. That pregnancy was brilliant. He didn't want to hurt you. I said you'd survive."

"How, Sonya?" she demanded. "You weren't leaving me anything."

"John insisted you have the house and your car."

Genny thought back to how she had invested her share of the family estate into their business. Surely John experienced some degree of guilt over stealing from her.

"And enough money to survive on until you worked things out," Sonya added.

The money she'd used to pay his debts, Genny realized. The money from the sale of her home and car. At first, she'd been so angry, upset that he'd left her alone and then because of his failure to plan for their future. "He loved me."

"Of course he did. Your safe world was a haven for him too. He came to me for excitement."

"But you're my sister."

Genny shivered at Sonya's malicious smile.

"As children, when you had something I wanted, I took it. If I asked, you handed it over even quicker." Sonya spat the words at her. "I wanted John. Him and the almost five hundred thousand."

The pain almost overwhelmed her. "Don't you. . . Haven't you ever cared about me? My son?"

"That baby ruined my life."

"Because he prevented you from having someone who didn't belong to you in the first place?"

"I wanted a baby too. If John hadn't been so determined to finish that one last project, we would have been gone long before you told him you were pregnant."

"So why not tell me the truth then?"

"I loved him. I believed I would win. He kept promising we would tell you. I never should have left that summer. John didn't want me to go."

Genny looked puzzled.

"He didn't. He wanted a wife. A family. Said it would be over if I went back to college. I didn't want to give him up, but I wasn't housewife material either. I intrigued him, and I used it to my advantage. Your son could have just as easily been mine.

"And if I'd had any idea how much he wanted a child, I'd have made sure it happened," Sonya added. "All he talked about was the baby. He nagged. I threatened, and in the end he admitted he wanted his child more."

"Why tell me now?"

"Aren't you Christians always spouting off about how important the truth is?"

"Don't pretend righteousness, Sonya."

"Oh yes," she exclaimed, her blue eyes twinkling like jewels. "Nothing little Miss Perfect Genevieve ever did carried the same weight as Evil Sonya." Her resentful laugh ground out. "Bet you don't know the argument mother and father had that day started over me. I got into trouble, and mother was afraid my stupidity would hurt her career. Did you ever wonder why the idea of divorce didn't bother her? Because she had a bigger fish on the hook. I was at a friend's and saw her coming from her boyfriend's apartment. I wanted to confront her, but I stepped back inside and kept my mouth shut."

Secret lives. No wonder her parents led such a miserable existence. "So why are you angry with Stephen?"

"He doesn't like me," Sonya declared, slamming the pillow she held against the sofa. "I'm invisible to him."

Realization dawned. "It piques your pride that he's not interested in you?"

"Don't let your mockery of a marriage to John destroy the real thing you could have with Stephen. That man loves you. He plans to spend the rest of his days with one woman. You've got him wondering if you'll ever forget John. I figured the truth would make your decision easier. I won't lie and say I'm sorry, because I'd do it again."

"John didn't turn to you out of love," Genny said softly, confident she knew what drove her husband to Sonya.

"Don't be so sure of it, little sister."

"Did he talk? Did he mention the anxiety, the inadequacy, the unease?" Genny asked. "It was there. Every time another month passed."

"It wasn't his fault," Sonya defended. "You weren't fit to be his wife. He deserved better."

"Maybe," Genny agreed. The sting of the words brought back the doubts, her plans for a future with Stephen. "Maybe it's all true. But at least his son was more important to John than you."

"Touché, little sister. I wondered if you'd ever show any Kelly spunk. You're too kind and sensitive to be believed."

"It's part of me, Sonya. And it won't go away because two people I loved let me down. I defended you when no one else in the world would. Now I understand why I was the only one.

"I thought you needed love. That you were suffering because of the past. Our parents were so dedicated to their own needs they forgot they had children. Why should I think my sister would be any different? You're worse than they ever dared to be. You helped yourself to my husband, a husband who could set aside his cheating for the child I carried.

"And you made me feel like a burden," Genny accused. "Every time I mentioned money, all that time, knowing you'd stolen every cent from me. . ."

Sonya shrugged carelessly. "But you've landed on your feet. Why shouldn't I?"

"It's always you," Genny said, coming to her feet. Words, long bottled deep inside, surged to her lips. "Your selfish needs come first. Maybe I am a silly, insecure burden, but your derision and ridicule haven't destroyed me. I won't give you the opportunity to try again." Genny jerked the door open and started outside. She stopped to share her final words on the subject. "Consider the money you stole from my son payment for staying away from us forever."

"You'll forgive me," Sonya sneered. "You won't be able to help yourself."

"I already have," Genny said, taunting Sonya with the truth. "You're really bothered that a plain woman like myself found two men to love her.

"John played with you, but I wore his ring. He may have run to you for excitement, but he found peace with me. You should consider what you offer a man. Looks fade, and when they do, what will you have left?

"I love Stephen and he loves me," Genny announced confidently. "I intend to become a woman he's proud to have in his life. I may never be a beauty, but you're living proof that beauty is only skin-deep. The heart is where real beauty lies, and you don't possess one."

"You'll need me again."

"No." There was no doubt in Genny's vehement response. "I'll accept charity and live on the street if need be, but I'll never take anything from you again. Simply because you never give. You begrudge and expect homage for every gesture. Not once in your entire life have you shown charitable kindness or love. I hope you can be happy with yourself because unless you change, you'll never find anyone to love you. Men may put beauty up on a pedestal, but they want a heart when they seek love."

Genny walked out the door.

※

The lights of home burned brightly, illuminating her way back to the man who loved her for herself. Anger didn't take away the lingering hurt. John was gone, but she had loved him, and knowing he planned to run away with Sonya intensified Genny's insecurities.

She could only wonder what kind of love she had shared with her child's father. A wry smile touched Genny's lips. She didn't want to feel satisfaction at destroying her sister's pleasure, but she was only human. The comment about his son being more important had hit the mark.

Stephen met her at the door. "How did it go? Everything okay?"

She swiped away the tears. "Just hold me."

Genny reveled in his loving embrace, knowing here was a man who considered her needs before his own. His hands soothed her back as he whispered gentle words of reassurance in her ear.

"Sonya told me she and John were going to run away together." Her voice cracked with pain as she added, "Jonathan was the reason he didn't go."

"Oh, Honey," he whispered, holding her closer. "I'm sorry."

"Me too. For many things. You saw the real Sonya. Maybe I did too, but I didn't want to believe the truth. She's all the family I have. I had no idea how much she resented me, how cruel she could be. She took great pleasure in telling me about John's infidelity. But she claims she told me so I'd see how much you love me."

"You still need her, Hon."

"I owe her. Sonya helped me realize I'm in danger of losing something more precious to me than I ever dreamed possible. I still have a lot of things to prove to myself, but no woman should reject the love of a man who loves her for herself.

"Remember I told you God uses us wherever we are. He made you my protector the night Jonathan was born. On the way home tonight, I thought about how short life is. I've wasted days refusing to accept what God intends for me. I want us to be married as soon as possible."

Stephen toned down his hurrah for the sake of the sleeping baby, but Genny knew he felt the same victory she did. Whatever life handed out, they would face it together, and the world would be a more wonderful place because two people believed in the miracle of God's love.

epilogue

"Genevieve Camden, stop arguing with me and breathe," Stephen instructed with mock severity, a glint of laughter in his gray eyes.

She touched his face. "What would your fans say if they could see you now?"

"I happen to think this outfit suits me perfectly. I'm considering auditioning for television's next heartthrob doctor role."

Genny snorted. "That color does nothing for you, and scrubs are hardly the attire of a well-loved singer noted for his romantic ballads. One who, I might add, should be at his awards ceremony."

"What could be more romantic than this? I'm exactly where I want to be," he said, bringing her hand to his lips. "Besides, I don't have a single female fan who would consider me hero material if I were there instead of here."

"You think they've forgiven you for marrying me?"

Stephen nodded agreement, his smile disappearing. Tension filled him when her eyes began to glaze over with the pain of another contraction.

Just as he had done with her every objection, Stephen used words to make Genny realize what God wanted for her. Even after admitting her love for him, she had her doubts she could be woman enough for him if she hadn't been for John. Stephen laughed outright at that, telling her he couldn't handle any more woman than her.

He pressed on about the landscaping business, forcing her to admit it was what she wanted and continued until she agreed to let him to finance the venture, all legal and with interest. She hoped to get several of Genny's Flower Gardens in the ground over the next year.

Of course it might be a bit difficult with a toddler and newborn in tow. That part of her plan had not changed. After God, her marriage and children were her first priorities.

She'd pushed Stephen into revealing his true feelings about Bobby, even to the point that he admitted his reasons for doing so much at first had been to make amends for the loss of his young friend. Genny believed Stephen when he said that changed when he fell in love with her.

And in that way of his, Stephen found a way around most of her arguments. Love made her putty in his hands, and he knew it, sweeping her off her feet before she could object to his plans.

Their wedding ceremony took place one Sunday morning after church services, a very low-key, informal occasion for friends and family. Genny met Stephen's family for the first time on the day of their wedding and immediately adored them. His mother claimed her as a daughter, and they visited often.

Fearful Sonya would sell the news to a tabloid, Genny hesitated over inviting her sister. Sonya kept their secret but didn't attend the ceremony.

She and Stephen, along with the entire congregation of their church, prayed for Sonya with the hope that she would one day submit to the will of her Lord and Savior. Genny prayed to make her peace with her sister.

Stephen was dedicated to protecting their privacy and keeping them out of the limelight. She forgave him for the one time he slipped up. Too excited to wait until he returned home to share the news, Genny and Jonathan flew to where the band was performing and went backstage. Stephen dragged them out onstage and introduced the loves of his life. The fans cheered with him when he shared their wonderful news.

Much to her dismay, Dr. Rainer had agreed she wasn't getting any younger.

She still felt the loneliness, particularly after waving goodbye to Stephen, but she never felt neglected. Genny never had the slightest doubt he would come home to them.

At fifteen months, Jonathan was a beautiful child. Together they watched him grow, and Stephen teased her mercilessly when his first word was Daddy. Of course that was only right since he pursued Stephen with steadfast determination, moving as fast as his tiny legs would carry him.

At times she thought they'd never have another private moment, her dear friend, Ronnie, whisked Jonathan away for a special play date.

Ronnie and Slay loved him, and Genny trusted them with the confidence of a woman who knew her friends would never allow her child to come to harm. She returned the favor, baby-sitting Randy Jr. when they needed time alone.

Stephen recorded his solo album. After many months, it remained at the top of the Christian music charts. Every time they received a piece of fan mail witnessing the blessings his music brought to believers and nonbelievers, Stephen said he had made the right decision.

She squeezed his hand as the pain encompassed her body. "Stephen!"

"I think this was where I came in," he joked, leaning to kiss her forehead. "Now focus and breathe."

"I told you I was too old," Genny said, panting with the contraction.

"You don't get pregnant and then decide you're too old. It's not the natural order of things."

"Natural order, indeed. If I didn't love you so much. . ."

He grinned and wiped her brow. "Well, Doc has assured me you're in perfect health. Better than some of his twenty-year-old patients. I think he's even more surprised that this baby isn't premature. Right, Doc?"

Dr. Rainer looked at him. "With your lifestyle, yes. Stephen, you really shouldn't argue with Genny right now."

"Right," Stephen agreed good-naturedly. "Did I tell you you're having a—"

"Baby," Genny supplied, tightening her hold on his hand.

"You don't have to break my fingers."

"I'll break more than that if you spoil my surprise."

"You said the S word," Stephen teased. "You must be delirious with pain."

"I suppose I'll never hear the end of it if I admit to liking your surprises."

"Nor see the end of them," he said with a quick kiss.

"Okay, you two. Let's get this over with. I want my dinner," Dr. Rainer called.

"Cruel." The word left Genny in a whispered cry as she followed his instruction.

Things sped up and in a matter of minutes, a perfectly healthy baby girl lay in Stephen's arms. "Her mother's eyes," he whispered.

"Her daddy's lungs," Genny added, marveling at the baby's lusty cries. The heart-rending tenderness with which Stephen stared down at his daughter brought tears to her eyes.

"I love you," Stephen said as he leaned to give Genny a glimpse of their child. "She's beautiful."

"What else would you expect of Stephanie Camden?"

"Other than perfection?" he suggested.

Genny smiled and lifted a hand to his face. Stephen had been right. Perfection was the pinnacle, but if their life together got any more perfect, she wasn't sure she'd survive it.

A Letter To Our Readers

Dear Reader:

In order that we might better contribute to your reading enjoyment, we would appreciate your taking a few minutes to respond to the following questions. We welcome your comments and read each form and letter we receive. When completed, please return to the following:

Fiction Editor
Heartsong Presents
PO Box 719
Uhrichsville, Ohio 44683

1. Did you enjoy reading *Close Enough to Perfect* by Terry Fowler?
   ❏ Very much! I would like to see more books by this author!
   ❏ Moderately. I would have enjoyed it more if

   _____

   _____

   _____

2. Are you a member of **Heartsong Presents**?   ❏ Yes   ❏ No
   If no, where did you purchase this book? _____

   _____

3. How would you rate, on a scale from 1 (poor) to 5 (superior),
   the cover design? _____

4. On a scale from 1 (poor) to 10 (superior), please rate the
   following elements.

   _____ Heroine   _____ Plot
   _____ Hero   _____ Inspirational theme
   _____ Setting   _____ Secondary characters

5. These characters were special because?_____

_____

_____

6. How has this book inspired your life?_____

_____

_____

7. What settings would you like to see covered in future
   Heartsong Presents books? _____

_____

_____

8. What are some inspirational themes you would like to see
   treated in future books? _____

_____

_____

9. Would you be interested in reading other **Heartsong
   Presents** titles? ❑ Yes ❑ No

10. Please check your age range:
     ❑ Under 18   ❑ 18-24
     ❑ 25-34   ❑ 35-45
     ❑ 46-55   ❑ Over 55

Name_____

Occupation _____

Address _____

City_____ State_____ Zip_____